OTHER GREAT TIT

DISCIPL
DISCIPLIN
(Also available titl

MW00899434

BEYOND DOMESTIC DISCIPLINE

THE MANOR HOUSE
First Year
Second Year
The Farm
The Council of Thirteen
Captured
Heart Manor

THE PARTY SERIES
The Party Of eight
The Party of Four

THE ROLE PLAY PARTIES
School and Medical Themes
Maid and Prisoner Themes

THE SUBMISSION PARTIES
Book One

DARKMORE PRISON

THE DETECTIVE SERIES
STOLEN
ENVY
GLUTTONY
GREED/WRATH
SLOTH
PRIDE

THE SERVANT WIFE
THE SISTER SERVANT WIFE
SLAVE CAMP

TRUE LOVE NEVER DIES

EVILNEZER

SPANKING IN SUBURBIA

With thanks to all at

A Domestic Discipline Society (ADDS)

For the wealth of information available and a truly wonderful bunch of people in the chat room; without whom this book would not have been possible.

http://adomesticdisciplinesociety.blogspot.co.uk

Contents

*

CHAPTER ONE

As Lisa approached her front door, she could feel the tension of the day across the back of her shoulders and neck. It was a typical day, as in a crappy one! Her boss was a jerk, a bully who thought he was funny making her work another weekend on someone else's project; "Because they were not up to running an implementation weekend," for fuck's sake and to cap it all, the trains had been delayed, again! She was tired and irritable.

Opening the door, she could smell dinner in the oven and coffee brewing. She shrugged off her coat and shoes and went through into the lounge, not even calling out hello as she passed the kitchen where her partner, John, was. John followed her into the lounge.

'Hello, love. How was your day?'

He placed a hot cup of coffee on the table for her and gave her a kiss, and squeezed her shoulder.

'Fine!' she snapped.

John quietly left the room, leaving Lisa tense, cross, upset, but most of all, guilty. John had done nothing. She was wrong to snap at him, but she just could not stop herself. She felt all these emotions just seething around inside of her and she took it out on him. She knew she was pushing him away. She knew they were teetering on the edge of complete collapse, but she just couldn't seem to stop herself. She wanted him to stop her, to take charge and stop her, but she would never accept any

6

type of violence towards her and when he raised his voice, she knew he would not back it up with any show of force; which she loved him for, but it also allowed her to simply yell back louder. He was a great guy, a fantastic catch. Everyone said so, and she said so frequently. Bastard, she thought without rancour.

John called out from the kitchen.

'I've run you a nice hot bath, go soak, relax and I'll be up in a minute with a glass of wine. Dinner won't be for an hour or so yet, so no rush.'

Lisa felt a rush of emotion; she thought she was going to cry. That was perfect, just what she needed. She loved him, she knew that. *Bloody bastard*, she thought with a touch of self mockery. She wanted to hate him, have a focus for her anger, her unhappiness, and he made it hard for that to be him when he was so considerate, so loving. *Selfish bastard.*

Lisa grabbed her purse and went upstairs, unable to offer a conciliatory word or even thanks, and guilt settled on her like a blanket. The guilt made her angry, the anger made her defensive. When her defences were up; it made her act like a bitch. She felt like she was spiralling out of control, sometimes the pressure inside built to where it felt like she would burst, which usually resulted in a blazing row with John.

As she removed her clothes, flinging them onto the bed, she felt some of her tensions fade. Opening the door to the bathroom, the fragrances of the bath bombs wafted around her, soothing her. The heat of the water enveloped her in a warm embrace. The soft lights of the candles flickered in the draft she had created. It was perfect. *Total Bastard*, she thought with a smile.

Lowering herself into the bath, the hot water instantly eased her shoulders and her mind. Her eyes closed, and she lay, finally relaxing, unwinding from her day. She heard John come in, and the clink as he placed a wineglass on the side of the bath. She knew she should say something, anything to bridge that small crack she had created downstairs, something simple, anything, anything nice that is, but her pride would not let her. In truth, she feared if she let go, even just a little, she would not be able to hold it together. So she stayed silent, kept her eyes closed, and pretended she was unaware of his presence. She heard the door quietly close as a tear escaped and ran down her cheek.

Her mind turned over the events at work. The guilt she felt turned to anger. Thoughts of her day crowded her mind. She played the conversation with her boss repeatedly in her mind, where she had pointed out the Project Manager he had appointed was not doing her job, was not on the ball and was definitely not ready for implementation of the software that weekend. He had blamed her, told her she would run the weekend implementation because the other project manager did not have the right skill set for such a task. Lisa fumed. It was so unfair. She had her own projects and now she had to cover for another, on a weekend no less, and to cap it all there would be no management support what so ever. It was a total carve up, and she knew it. Worse, she had not refused, and she knew, deep down, she was disappointed with herself for not doing so. Frustrated at being trapped in a job she needed and wanted, but with a boss who used his position to intimidate her. Her anger boiled, and she got out of the bath, dried, shrugged on a bathrobe and sat on the bed, waiting for John to call up when dinner was ready.

Dinner was the same tense affair it had become lately. John tried to engage her in conversation, about her work, about the book she was reading; he'd talk about his day, anything to get a conversation started, all of which were met with curt responses, often just a word or two, snappy or sarcastic. Which was worse, as the guilt would set in and then the anger which she would try to hold inside, then the defences, then the silence.

For the rest of the meal; silence.

John started clearing away the plates and Lisa offered to do the washing up, so he left them on the side and put the kettle on. He brought back two hot cups of tea and some cake he made earlier in the day and they sat congenially enough together, watching some TV. They both liked a reality show and enjoyed commenting and debating the trials and tribulations these rich folks had with their cheating ways. It broke the ice between them. John reached over and squeezed Lisa's hand and she squeezed it back and soon they were laughing and joking together about the antics of one or other of the cast. He loved her; she knew that, without any doubt. And she loved him; she just had to work out how not to take her irritations and frustrations out on him as it was damaging them, tearing them apart.

Lisa went up to bed early. She usually did these days to avoid John when he turned in. As he sat in front of the TV, watching sports, she slipped upstairs without saying good night and got into bed. After a few minutes, tossing and turning, it was clear she would not sleep anytime soon, so she switched on her laptop, her fingers tapping the sides, waiting for the thing to boot up. Finally, she thought, entering her favourite website for erotic stories into the search engine. Rather than go straight to the home page of the site as usual, she was offered a list of websites. Letting out a huge sigh in frustration, she went to retype the site name, seeing that she had misspelt it the first time around, when something caught her eye.

Q: What is a Domestic Discipline relationship?

A: Domestic Discipline is something that can and does work for many couples

Intrigued, she entered Domestic Discipline into the search engine and started to read. The more she read, the more she felt a connection and the more she wanted to find out.

Domestic Discipline refers to an agreement of rules and penalties between two partners as a corrective measure for specific misbehaviours. It serves to encourage and preserve a harmonious and stable home environment by providing the means to express displeasure and to address contentious issues related to a spouse's behaviour in a secure and controlled manner.

Ok, she thought, harmonious and stable home environment, perfect. A way to express displeasure and address contentious issues related to a spouse's behaviour in a controlled manner. Ok, that would relate to her behaviour and how John would express and deal with it. When she reread corrective measures for misbehaviours, she felt a tingle.

She was surprised by John climbing into bed with her, and she warmly returned his kiss and said,

'Good night, sleep well,' (and meant it) with barely a glance away from the screen. John smiled; surprised his wife was still up and returned his kiss, no less. It didn't take much to make him happy, just a contented wife, and he was done.

Lisa continued to read. Lots of books were available, but she wanted the information now, not to wait, so she continued to search and came across a website filled with links to blogs and articles about all things Domestic Discipline. She noticed the time and reluctantly switched off the laptop and put it away. As she snuggled under the duvet, words from one article title she'd read were fresh in her mind.

Spanking punishment, spanking discipline, spanking maintenance, spanking erotic.

For the first time in ages, her hand slipped between her thighs and within no time, she let out a sigh of pleasure and had one of the best night's sleeps she had had in a long time.

The following morning, she felt full of energy. She showered and greeted John warmly, even kissing him full on the mouth before taking her bowl of porridge and coffee through to the lounge. Her mind had instantly gone back to the night before and she was replaying what she had read over in her mind and was eager with anticipation to read more. Her day flew by, busy and stressful as usual, but nothing staying in her mind, festering as she prodded and dwelt on it, not today. Today her thoughts kept tumbling around words like *Discipline* and *Punishment* and *Spanking.*

On the platform waiting for her train, she didn't notice it was late, nor that she was too slow getting on to get a seat. Her mind was already racing ahead to when she got home and back onto the laptop. As she walked from the station to her home, she felt excited, eager; her feet seemed light as feathers as she made her way through the streets to her door. Entering, she called out a 'Hello' to John and hung her coat on the hook, kicked her shoes off and nudged them neatly together underneath, and went into the kitchen, smiling. She could not help herself. She was teasing herself, holding back from running up the stairs to her laptop. She gave John a kiss and took her cup of coffee from his hands and went into the lounge. She spoke about her day briefly, not dwelling on anything in particular, breezing over the issues and frustrations, not wanting to spoil her mood with work stuff. She asked about his day and smiled at the surprise that flashed momentarily across his face and warmed to the smile that followed. She watched the news whilst he finished making the dinner and they ate in companionable silence in between conversations. As he cleared the plates, she realised she hadn't washed up the night before like she had promised, and he hadn't said a word in rebuke. *Discipline, Punishment* and *Spanking*. It was as if a light bulb had gone off in her mind. She couldn't wait any longer and dashed upstairs to fire up her laptop. As her fingers tapped the casing, waiting for it to start up, John came into the room with a cup of tea and more of the cake he had made yesterday.

'What are you working on?'

'Just some research for a project I've just started.'

'OK, I'll leave you in peace, shout if you need anything.'

'Thanks, and thanks for the tea,' Lisa called out after him as he left the bedroom.

Lisa's attention was soon back to the screen as the website finally loaded and she clicked on that article, the one that had been teasing her mind all day.

Spanking punishment, spanking discipline, spanking maintenance, spanking erotic.

There was an old drawing of a woman over a man's knee and the article talked about spanking, but within a paragraph or two Lisa was losing the excitement she felt earlier. It was very informative, but she needed more. So she closed that window and looked again.

In the middle of the screen was

DD Chat Room

Review Rules before entering the Chat Room.

Lisa had never been in a chat room before, so was a little unsure, but took the plunge and clicked on the link, opening up the chat room for the first time.

CHAPTER TWO

LISA joined the chat

Trix: We occasionally include fun spankings, but there is a definite difference between fun and not.

Trix: Usually it's when he's trying to "persuade" me to get out of the nice warm comfy bed on a cold morning. ☺

Pat: Love swats are different lol.

Trix: Yeah, but they don't stay that way for long, Pat, not if I push it beyond a joke.

Pat: I bet. ☺

Trix: I usually don't though, and he knows that. He'll swat hard enough to sting slightly, but not harder than that, and then he'll sit back and promise a cuddle if I get up.

Pat: oooo.

Pat: Sounds so manipulative lol.

Peter: Lol the Stick and the Cuddle the DD version of the Stick and Carrot.

Trix: Hehe, it's fun for us, and all play.

Trix: We like those silly little games; he'll let me know if he's tired of playing, lol.

Trix: I'll get up far enough to swing around and put my head on his leg before announcing that I'm up.

Trix: Hi Lisa, and welcome.

Peter: Hi Lisa, welcome to DD chat, first time here?

LISA: Yes, just starting reading about DD yesterday.

Peter: Well, this is a great room, full of friendly folk, most of whom are living the DD lifestyle and happy to share their experiences and thoughts.

Pat: Welcome Lisa, are you thinking about being TiH or HoH?

LISA: I am not too sure of the terminology. What are TiH and HoH?

Peter: TiH (Taken in Hand) is the submissive partner; HoH (Head of House) is the dominant partner within the Domestic Discipline (DD) aspect.

LISA: Ok I would be TiH then. ☺

Peter: And do you have a partner, Lisa?

Pat: Have you mentioned your interest to your partner Lisa?

Peter: Lol. ☺

LISA: ☺ Yes, I have a partner, and no, I have not mentioned it yet. Just trying to understand what it involves. So far, it's connecting with me in a strong way, like finding the missing piece of a puzzle.

Trix: I specifically sought out a D/s/DD relationship; it was what I knew I wanted.

Pat: It found me. My Husband has been spanking me since we started as a couple; it's how we were both raised as well.

Peter: It does pose the Nature vs. Nurture question. Pat has always been spanked - nurture, whereas Trix wanted it in her relationship – nature.

Peter: I wonder if Pat had not been spanked from the beginning, would she have researched it and brought it to Graham later in their relationship?

Trix: I wasn't spanked as a kid though, occasionally smacked but not seriously spanked. So I have no idea why the need is there in me.

Trix: Maybe it's my submissive nature - that's always been there.

Pat: I was spanked by my mother through my middle teens.

Pat: One thing, it's nice to have someone who doesn't put up with my sh*t.

Pat: I like that strong sense of right and wrong.

Trix: So do I. I like the sense of boundaries, of accountability. One of the reasons I struggled the first time at University, I think, was that I didn't have that structure there and had to develop my own. I got decent marks, but still. . .

Trix: I wonder what would have happened had I found a Dom while I was in University.

Pat: Don't know Trix.

Trix: Neither do I, but it's interesting to wonder. I might have passed Physics and Statistics for a start. 🎁

Pat: lol.

Pat: How old were you when you decided to have a DD relationship?

Trix: I was about 18 when I discovered D/s and didn't seriously think about a relationship until I was about 22. Then I met L when I was 23.

Trix: And never looked back.

Trix: The odd thing was, I discovered D/s while looking for something completely different, lol.

Pat: I moved in with Graham when I was 17. I thought I was "big" enough to skip a day of school with my sister. Graham spanked us both when he came home early and caught us.

Trix: Ouch.

Trix: I've never skipped school; I liked it too much.

Peter: Did your sister get a second punishment from your mom when she got home?

Pat: We both did.

Peter: 🙁 ouch.

Pat: What were you looking for?

Trix: Something for an assignment. I forget which one now.

Trix: Then I got interested in D/s and forgot the assignment for that day. I picked it up the next day and finished it, but the first day was wasted on D/s research.

Trix: See why I think the idea of me having had a Dom while at University might have been interesting?

Pat: Trix, had you previously had any brushes with spanking before you met L?

Trix: Not really Pat, no.

Trix: Just fantasies. The reality is better, though.

Trix: I was just looking for something which validated how I felt. D/s spoke to me in a way that nothing else had up to then. And then last year I found DD.

Pat: Yes, it is. It's quite an adventure, like it or not.

Trix: Oh, I like the majority of it, Pat. The not so enjoyable bits are controllable by the way I behave. If I choose to misbehave, I have to accept the consequences that I've agreed to.

Tanya: I introduced it to my partner. We are a more traditional gay couple. Is that an issue here?

Jack and Jill: Not at all Tanya. As long as you have an interest in DD, everyone is welcome.

Tanya: good to hear.

Peter: Still here Lisa? Feel free just to sit and browse. Of course, if you have any questions please do not hesitate to ask.

LISA: ☺ Yes, still here. I am enjoying reading the conversation. I feel a little less 'crazy' than I did earlier. It seems so normal to be chatting about spankings and punishments in here.

Jack and Jill: Hi Lisa, yes, spanking is a totally normal conversation in here. lol.

Jack and Jill: What prompted you to bring it to your partner?

Tanya: I beat myself up a lot about things that I do wrong and I thought that maybe DD by accepting punishment, could help me get rid of those feelings of guilt.

Jack and Jill: That's understandable. That's part of the reason I asked for DD. I had trouble letting go of guilt.

Blush: In my case, I am very "Alpha" by nature, but I don't want to have to be in charge in a relationship with a Man.

Blush: Unfortunately, most men are too easy for me to push around even when I don't try to.

Jack and Jill: That seems to be the case a lot of times, Blush. I have a lot more respect for Jack now that he doesn't let me back him down.

Jack and Jill: I may fuss at times when he puts his foot down, but secretly I'm happy about it

Jack and Jill: I went through several of them before I found Jack. Even with him being different, it still took me 7 years before I brought DD to him.

Jack and Jill: It took me a while to figure out that's what I wanted.

Jack and Jill: Now that I have it, I can't imagine being in a different type of relationship.

Tanya: My partner is very much in charge of our relationship and always has been. I think this is a natural step for us. She was raised in a traditional way, typical of where she grew up, albeit with her Mom very much in charge.

Jack and Jill: That's good Tanya.

Blush: As long as you are both clear in your agreements about DD, I think it's very healthy Tanya.

LISA: How did you bring it to Jack, Jill?

Jack and Jill: I wrote him a 7 page email as to why I wanted DD in my life. Longest couple of hours of my life waiting for him to respond.

Tanya: Jill, how long have you been practicing DD?

Jack and Jill: almost 2 years now.

Jack and Jill: In some ways, Jack was always the HoH type. It just wasn't until we added DD and I stepped out of his way that he could finally step into the role.

Courtney joined the chat.

Blush: hi Courtney.

Jack and Jill: hi Courtney.

Courtney: hi.

Tanya: Do you feel like it has strengthened your relationship? Hi Courtney.

Jack and Jill: Definitely Tanya.

Jack and Jill: We talk a lot more now and not just about superficial things like what happened at work or what's going on with our daughter. And we definitely touch more.

LISA: I'd better get going. I had not realised it was so late. Thanks though, I feel a lot clearer about whether I should continue to explore this lifestyle.

Jerry: And will you continue, Lisa?

LISA: Oh yes. ☺

LISA: Left the chat.

CHAPTER THREE

The tensions of the day; she felt tired and irritable. As she opened the door, she smelt the dinner cooking and a pot of coffee freshly brewed, both welcoming smells. As she shrugged off her coat, she thought about her conversation in the chat room and the blogs that she had read and tried to calm her thoughts and enter a more submissive frame of mind. She called out;

'Hello,' and went through into the kitchen.

'Hi, hun,' John replied, handing her a cup of coffee. 'How was your day?'

'Typical shit,' she replied, feeling her irritability rise.

Sensing that was the wrong thing to chat about, John changed the subject.

'What do you fancy doing this weekend?'

'I don't know. Why don't you come up with something for once!' Lisa snapped. 'Why is it always up to me? You're fucking useless! Why the fuck did I marry you?'

Lisa slammed her cup down, spilling hot coffee over her hand, which only fuelled her anger even further.

'Fucking shit,' she yelled and stormed out of the kitchen, slamming the door back against the wall. She heard the "crack" and knew she had broken the glass panel in the door.

She went upstairs, her flash of anger already ebbing away, to be replaced by an overwhelming sense of guilt and sadness. She heard the front door close behind her. John had walked out. She felt loss; she felt abandoned, and she felt sad and lonely. She threw herself onto her bed and cried, feeling very sorry for herself but knowing she was largely to blame. Why had she snapped so quickly, so unreasonably? Why had she said those things? She loved John; they had been married for twenty-two years and he did everything. He took care of the house, the kids until they had left for college, finances; he even decided what they would do on the weekends, taking into account anything specific she needed, so why she had called him useless was beyond her. And the swearing, what would her Mother say to such filthy language? Back when she was a young girl, she knew exactly what her Mom would have said and she would have said it with a slipper and a bar of soap. She had to get her temper in hand and her swearing, my god, which had got way out of control. How she wished John had told her to fetch the slipper and taken her firmly into the lounge and over his knee.

As these thoughts became images in her mind, she felt herself tingle. She slid her hands down and pulled her at her skirt, trying to raise it, to pull it up her thighs so she could satisfy the itch that was starting to build. Frustrated, she reached behind and undid the clasp and the zip, fumbling as the urgency grew. Pushing her skirt down, she slipped her fingers into the waistband of her panties and pushed them down too, kicking her legs, trying to fling the garments off, to free her legs with an eagerness she had not felt in such a long while. In her haste she had not realised how close she had come to the edge of the bed, a realisation that hit home as she tumbled off, her legs finally free of her skirt. From the floor, one last kick saw the thin material of her panties fly through the air and land on the bedside lamp. As she sat up, she puffed some air out of the side of her mouth to blow away a lock of hair over one eye. A smile teased her lips as she pictured what that must have looked like. As she stood up, she felt the drafts of air she created cool against the wetness of her lips, reminding her of her needs. She jumped back on the bed and with no hesitation lay back, spread her legs wide and practically slapped her hands against her pussy in her desperation to calm the tingling demands. She closed her eyes and imagined the scene again, her yelling, swearing, banging the coffee cup down, and breaking the windowpane in the door. "Oh, my" her eyes flew open in a moment of shame and guilt, then the throbbing took hold and she lay back and resumed her thoughts.

John grabbed her around the arm, not hard or rough, but firm as he marched her into the lounge.

'That's about enough of that, young lady,' he said, calm, firm, and in charge.

He sits himself down and pulls her over his lap. His large hand rests on her bottom, holding her in place and letting her know of his intentions all in one move.

Lisa's hands were sliding over her lips, stroking her clit, sending ripples of pleasure through her body. Her legs opened wider as her body demanded more. She slipped one finger into her opening, then two. Usually two was enough for her, but not today. She slipped a third in and felt her opening stretch around her fingers, tight, a slight, satisfying sting, but still this was not enough. With a moan, she rolled over and reached for the bedside drawer. Tugging the drawer open, she searched inside by touch alone. Where was that fucking thing? She thought before her fingers touched the spongy sleeve of her favourite vibrator. Rolling it with her fingertips until she could get a good grip, she held it aloft triumphantly before guiding it between her thighs and into her pussy. It slid in easily. Gosh, I am *so* wet; she thought and when she realised she was on John's side of the bed and he'd get the wet patch, a soft giggle escaped. She didn't bother turning it on; it was not the vibrations she wanted this night, but the thick hard shaft. She closed her eyes, picturing herself over John's knee. His hand rises, the vibrator just touching her opening, the hand falls with a loud SMACK; the vibrator thrust hard into her pussy, causing her to gasp aloud.

*

John's hand rose and fell over and over as he spanked his wife's bottom.

'I think, young lady.'

SMACK, SMACK.

'It's about time.'

SMACK, SMACK,

'We addressed a few issues I have.'

SMACK, SMACK,

'Namely your attitude.'

SMACK.

'And your language.'

SMACK, SMACK, SMACK.

*

LISA's feet were flat on the bed, her knees acting as the pivot as she pushed her hips up to meet the hard thrust of the vibrator into her hot wet tunnel, her walls tight around the shaft but so slick with arousal they barely impeded its plunge into her body. Her arousal was building fast and her thrusts quickened; in her mind, John was spanking her harder and faster. Her moans and soft cries filled the air.

23

*

John reaches down and lifts her skirt up over her bottom, then slides his fingers under the edge of her panties, pulling them down her thighs, so effortlessly, so commandingly. Now his hand is spanking her bare bottom, harder and faster. Lisa blushes at her predicament, bent over John's lap. Getting her bare bottom spanked was embarrassing enough, but she also felt the coolness of the air against her lips. She was wet, so very, very wet.

*

I must be going crazy to want this, she thought.

*

'I am going to make sure this is a lesson you will not forget in a hurry, Lisa.'

SMACK, SMACK, SMACK.

*

LISA was pounding the vibrator with one hand and rubbing her clit so hard sparks of pain mingled with the waves of pleasure.

*

John continued to spank her bottom until it was a rosy red, then he told her to stand and remove all of her clothing. Lisa blushed furiously. John had seen her naked thousands of times but this felt different, being told to strip, to stand naked in front of him, hands on her head, so embarrassing, so arousing. The throbbing of her bottom, the hot stinging of her cheeks, kept this from being a sex game. She felt properly humbled and ashamed of her behaviour. The tension and bad temper had left, and her body now called for something more intimate. But it was clear her punishment was not over.

24

'Now, young lady, we have to address that foul language of yours','

He produced a bar of ivory soap and slowly unwrapped it. Lisa felt her eyes going wide, memories of her childhood flooding back. That horrible taste of soap teased her memory so vividly she felt like she could actually taste it.

'Open,' was all he said, one word of command.

All thoughts of arguing, refusing, begging for anything, but the soap flew away with that one word. Lisa opened her mouth wide and John placed the bar between her teeth.

'Now go and stand in the corner until I call you.'

Lisa obeyed, the soap warmed by his hand, soft enough for her teeth to sink into it. The hard surface slowly turned to paste within her mouth.

*

She was getting close, but she was not ready to come. Her punishment had not played out fully in her mind and she needed it, too. She needed to be punished for her behaviour. She didn't stop or slow her actions, though; her proper punishment was to deny herself the pleasure for as long as she could. Her fingers twisted the skin around her clit, gripping it hard and grinding it until the sparks of pain leapt like dolphins within the waves of her pleasure. She thrust harder, jamming the vibrator into her pussy.

*

15 minutes she waited. 15 long minutes with that horrible yucky soap causing a burning sensation in the back of her throat. She knew John would not let her come to any harm. That was the essence of punishment within DD. It hurt, yes, but it did no harm. John came to her when her time was up. She felt his arms envelop her, hold her tight as he whispered, 'I love you so much.' He took the bar of soap from her lips and she turned into his arms, whispering back;

'I'm sorry, John, so sorry.'

John sssshed her; telling her she was forgiven. That she had accepted her punishment and now it was all over. She hugged him tight and, with a twinkle in her eye, kissed him passionately, her tongue darting into his mouth, surprising him with a taste of soap. He kissed her back hard, although he also growled from the back of his throat, causing her to break the kiss and laugh, a light, delightful laugh of merriment and mischief.

*

Her arousal climbed and climbed until it reached its tipping point. It teetered there, teasing her, tormenting her. In her mind the sounds of John's hand against her bottom were loud, so loud she could have sworn she heard the slap as her orgasm crashed through her body, tumbling down from heights hitherto unknown, washing through her body on one long wave of pleasure, quickly followed by another and another. As her climax ebbed and fade away, a soft lassitude replaced it, sending her off to sleep.

When she awoke, it was dark out. She climbed off the bed and slipped on a bathrobe before heading downstairs. Her pussy gave a delightful ache of abuse, which sent tingles throughout her body.

She went to the kitchen first, to find the stove cold and pots and pans of food, half cooked, sitting in tepid water, left untouched. She felt a wave of sadness and guilt wash over her. She gave herself a shake. She knew for sure what she had to do and that she had to make a change within herself, to make the changes in their relationship she knew were needed.

She went into the lounge to find John sitting quietly, watching a soccer game on the telly. She sat on the sofa next to him, curled herself into a ball and fell into him, placing her head into his lap, muttering softly,

'Sorry.'

She felt him relax; his hand gently lands on her head and stroked her hair.

'Me too.'

She knew he had nothing to apologise for but was warmed by it, anyway. She snuggled deeper into his lap and slipped her arm around his waist to hug him. She felt him responded beneath her cheek and she smiled to herself. Slipping her arm free, she quickly undid his button and zip, realising what a practiced hand she had become at releasing "the snake" from a pair of trousers. She fought down the urge to giggle. That same experience had taught her how fragile the male ego was about their penis and giggling at the wrong moment could so kill the mood. His penis, however, sprung eagerly into her hand and she wasted no time slipping her mouth over the head, already looking fit to burst as it continued to grow. She used all her techniques, running through them quickly as now her own body craved some attention. She grasped his shaft firmly and pumped hard and fast two, three, four times, then she slipped her mouth over the top again, using her tongue to coat it with saliva to act as a lubricant for her fingers, which she now used to slip over the top of his cock, teasing the pleasure point just at its base, continuing to lick to keep it wet. She regretted not having a proper lubricant because then she could have really driven him mad with desire. That was so much fun, but now was not the time. And time was a factor with most men. She slid her fingers up and down his shaft slowly, so slowly, delighting in the moans she was eliciting, before taking him completely by surprise and sitting up, not knowing she was millimetres from smacking him in the face with the back of head, so quick were her movements. Before he had time to think, to react, to lose control, his penis was buried to its hilt inside her pussy. As she sunk down on his cock, she felt the soft protests of her bruised tunnel and she shivered. It felt so good. Like a spanked bottom the following morning, she thought to herself. She lifted herself ever so slowly up his shaft. Kissing him full mouthed on the lips, she let her hips drop sharply, thrusting downwards, causing another moan of pleasure. She did this four, five times before he growled, grabbed her bottom with both hands and thrust upwards. Past the point of no return, she could feel his hardness thrusting inside her. Her over sensitised lining could feel the force of his orgasm and its hot wetness as it flooded her insides, barely contrasting against her own hot, wet desire, but just enough to feel it.

They curled up together as he watched the rest of the game, her thoughts already working out how to progress her research and figure out how to talk to John about Domestic Discipline.

CHAPTER FOUR

LISA joined the chat.

Lynette: joined the chat.

David: Hi Lisa.

LISA: Hello David.

David: I haven't seen your name before - new here?

LISA: Yes, only been here a couple of times so far.

David: Welcome - what brings you?

LISA: Thank you; I have been curious for some time. Found the site by accident, a happy accident.

David: If I can answer any questions. . . .

LISA: Awww thanks, I am not even sure where to start.

David: Do you have a preference as to which role would be yours?

LISA: Yes Taken In Hand, the receiving end: right?

David: Do you have someone in mind to be your HoH?

LISA: I am married and would love my husband to be HoH, though I am not sure how he will take to it.

David: I am TiH to my wife who is HoH.

LISA: You might be a good person to talk to then, since you would understand what I want.

David: I was in the same situation - my wife is not naturally dominant.

LISA: But now she is?

David: I would not say dominant, but she has seen the positive effect it has had on our relationship.

David: And she has grown quite comfortable with the use of a hairbrush on a bare bottom.

LISA: That's good.

David: The relationship has two components - the authority aspect and the actual discipline aspect.

LISA: We have played with it as fun or sexual and that is not what I want or desperately need.

David: In a way though, that's good - he'll grow into it.

David: Right - we 'played' for several years.

David: Last summer I took a deep breath and explained that I wanted it to be 'real.'

David: Not an easy conversation.

LISA: How did that go?

David: We had the conversation that every TiH ends up having - "I don't want to hurt you."

LISA: He will say the same thing to me. What's the difference between BDSM and DD?

David: Lisa - there is a difference between BDSM and DD in terms of the nature of what actually takes place.

David: BDSM can branch into many more ways of inflicting pain, which is not what DD is all about.

David: So back to the topic - we've all been through what you're looking at right now - how to get your spouse to take on the role of HoH.

LISA: Yes.

LISA: I feel like I am asking for a lot.

David: One thing is for sure - they can't read minds - you have to take a chance and say what you want.

Lynette: It is a lot; HoH is a tough job but we give them a great gift – ourselves.

LISA: Yes, I get what you both just said. I need to talk more to him.

David: The more experienced people here will all tell you that communication is at the heart of it.

LISA: ok.

Lynette: Some need to go slow. They don't all say on Saturday, tomorrow we start DD and then go full out.

David: If you go down this road, there are two more things that are important.

LISA: Good point. . . What's that David?

David: 1 - this has probably been in YOUR mind all your life - for him it's new.

David: You need to be patient and let him catch up.

LISA: Soooo very true.

David: 2 - If you want him to be more dominant, you must first be more submissive - to his will.

David: I'll give you an example.

David: I wanted my wife to lay down a bunch of rules and enforce them with strict discipline.

LISA: Ok.

David: As she thought things over, she said, "If we're going to do this - we're going to do it MY way."

David: She doesn't' want to be a "rules cop."

LISA: Ok, that makes sense.

David: So she decided that every Friday night things will be 'settled up' with the hairbrush.

David: It freed her from having to decide what infraction should result in immediate discipline or what could wait.

David: At first, I thought "this isn't how I imagined it."

David: But then I realized I had conceded control to her - so things are done her way.

LISA: Ohhh ok.

David: She's the HoH, so things are done her way.

David: It also avoids issues of 'consistency' for us - she never misses a Friday night hairbrush session, it seems.

Lynette: She probably looks as forward to them as you do.

Lynette: There is no right or wrong way to do DD - it's as individual as the couple. It's gotta be your own.

LISA: That is an issue here too. But like you said, it takes time.

LISA: This might be a silly question or too personal, so say so if it is, please. Does she do it until it really hurts, or a certain amount of time?

David: She puts a lowlight on so she can see as the skin gets red - she goes until she is satisfied with the effects.

LISA: Oh ok.

Lynette: It's not silly, but every HoH decides how it's administered. Some use a number of swats, some an amount of time, others until they feel the lesson is learned.

LISA: Ok thanks Lynette.

Lynette: One thing is true for all - they hurt!!

LISA: And, David, you said other things like lines and corner time?

David: We only have one rule (bedtime) and after the first time I got extra for missing it, I've never missed it again (so a good spanking works in my case).

David: Lynette is so right - a real spanking does really hurt.

Lynette: Lines, essays, corner time (which I hate), loss of privileges.

LISA: I can be a bit of a brat, have been running amuck too long.

Lynette: Fantasy spanking don't hurt - real spankings do.

LISA: I have high pain tolerance and I think that might scare the hubby.

Lynette: I have a pretty high pain tolerance also, but when he gets going, I can't hold still.

Lynette: I've lost computer time and frequent the corner.

LISA: Oh man, losing computer time would make me act right. LOL.

Lynette: That one did have its desired effect. But thankfully, he's only done it once.

Christine: Lol.

Christine: Mine has gotten better at the pull the car over method.

LISA: Christine, seriously pull the car over?

LISA: Does that embarrass you at all?

Christine: oh ya.

Christine: It's horrible. I was totally embarrassed at the time, getting spanked on the roadside like that. Several cars honked their horns as they drove by. But I am also a little in awe of him too; proud that he cared that much about my behaviour. Which sounds crazy to say, but it's true nevertheless.

Lynette: I think I'd behave in the car.

Christine: I have to say good nite HoH orders. See you guys later maybe.

LISA: Night.

Lynette: Nite Christine.

David: Lynette - when it's about to happen you think "why did I ask for this" - later (when you feel so cared for) you know why.

LISA: Yeah, there is love and caring in the discipline, I do know that.

Lynette: So true David.

Lynette: After 20 years of marriage, presenting myself naked to be spanked is embarrassing.

David: And I think a spanking is supposed to be embarrassing.

LISA: Hmmmm ok.

Lynette: Ok I'm going to bed nite all.

David: Nite Lynette.

LISA: Night Lynette, thank you.

David: You'll have to trust that he loves you and wants to give you what you need - the trick is to be honest (easier said than done).

LISA: Oh ok good idea.

David: One thing I DID do was stop trying to actually figure out why I want this - just makes you crazy - you'll know if it turns out that it isn't what you actually need.

LISA: I feel like I know why. I think so anyway.

David: Then you're ahead of most of us.

David: Something that many people here have tried is to write a letter or email.

LISA: Write an email saying what they want?

David: I've seen a lot of discussion about "I left it for him to read."

David: Yes - instead of having a conversation about it or to initiate one.

LISA: I can see that maybe as a way to get thoughts out because you can edit, get it straight in your head and on the paper without getting tongue tied.

David: What I did was write things out - but then sat with her and read through it together.

LISA: Good idea.

David: It was the long 4th of July weekend, and I just kept at it (nothing to lose once you start the conversation)

David: The one administering the spanking has the leverage though - he'll be able to control you.

LISA: Ok.

David: She has me lay over one knee, her sitting at the edge of the bed. My one arm is behind her back, and she takes hold of the other wrist.

LISA: *Nods* ok.

David: When I can't keep my legs down, she locks her other leg over - you really are helpless.

LISA: So, do you feel this has helped you improve in whatever way it was you wanted to improve?

David: What it did was to bring us to a level of intimacy and communication that had us like newlyweds after 30+ years.

LISA: Awwwww that is sweet.

David: Friends and family were asking if we'd done a marriage encounter or something.

LISA: That's good.

David: Yes - it is - life has never been better for us.

David: How hard do you want it to be?

LISA: Hard as in the spankings?

David: Yes.

LISA: I think it needs to be hard enough that it hurts. It has to be real.

LISA: The sting has never lasted thus far, so it needs to last.

David: Can I make a suggestion?

LISA: Of course.

David: Go to the store - in the ethnic hair care section, they have some good solid wooden hairbrushes.

LISA: I wondered where you got one of those. LOL.

David: It has the weight to impart a deep burn without him having to strike you very hard.

LISA: Great, thank you.

David: The other thing I would do if I were you is wear a pair of thin nylon panties and have him spank you over those.

LISA: Why the panties?

David: He won't be as concerned with the marks left by the hairbrush if he can't see them.

LISA: Oh ok.

David: But - believe me - they won't give your behind much protection.

David: There have been a couple of times when I've had some marks the next day (I didn't show them to her - I didn't want to scare her).

LISA: LOL.

David: You'll get a good spanking.

David: Whatever you do - resist the urge to 'coach' him afterwards - let him develop a sense of competence.

LISA: That will be hard for me.

David: But you have to do it - men need to feel competent - after all, if we won't ask for directions in the car, do you really think we're going to ask how to spank someone?

LISA: LOL good point.

David: My wife sort of asked a couple of times - I told her I could handle a bit more.

David: Actually, that led to a bit of a surprise.

LISA: Oh?

David: She decided to set up a safe word.

David: At first she didn't like that idea - she said I could just get away if I really needed to.

David: But then she decided that it was better to have a safe word - if I don't say her name, then she knows to ignore whatever I might say.

LISA: Have you ever had to use it?

David: I haven't used it so far.

LISA: How long have you been doing this?

David: Coming up on a year.

LISA: Cool.

David: Here's the thing - he undoubtedly cares about you a lot - he will have trouble with the idea of really giving you a good spanking - until he learns that he's not harming you though he WILL be hurting you temporarily.

David: You'll have to protect him as he comes up that learning curve.

David: Protect both his ego; I'm good at giving my wife what she needs, and his concerns about harming you.

LISA: Ok.

David: One last thing, if I may?

LISA: Sure.

David: You've been very frank and I think you are similar in your needs to me.

LISA: I figure why mess around, get to the point.

David: Some people here want the various forms of discipline to be equally distributed - some really need just spanking.

David: Some want extensive lists of rules - others don't.

LISA: I am open to other forms of punishment, but I think spankings would work for me more, perhaps in combination.

David: You'll find that some things sound right to you (fit with what you need).

David: And some don't.

LISA: I think I want a list of rules. Not sure.

David: I thought I did - but what I really wanted was for my wife to take the HoH role.

LISA: That I can understand. I feel it I am the HoH in some respects.

David: She has set this up for us in a way that works for her and that means that it works for me.

LISA: But I also want that very much.

LISA: That will be hard to give over control. Which is funny since that is part of what this is about.

David: I stopped trying to 'top from the bottom' and have let her set the pace.

LISA: I can see myself trying to top from the bottom as well.

David: No Kidding - in so many ways, the TiH is the stronger of the two, which is totally backwards.

LISA: I actually have tried that a little, to be more submissive.

David: Many of us are anything but submissive in the outside world.

David: I'm in the top mgt. of a 100m$ company - but when I get home, she's in charge - it feels so relaxing.

LISA: Interesting. I am hoping it will help me be more settled, more in control of myself, and more connected to John.

David: That's how it works for me.

David: Safe is a word you'll hear a lot around here.

David: Cared for as well.

LISA: LOL ok good.

LISA: Glad we speak the same language.

David: I hope I've helped some - you'll have to tell him what it is you really need - it's scary to leave yourself wide open, but it's what works.

LISA: You helped tremendously.

David: I'm going to call it a night. See you again, I hope.

LISA: Ok, thank you so very much.

LISA: Night.

LISA left the chat.

CHAPTER FIVE

The following morning, Lisa woke and decided today was the day. She switched off her alarm and quickly snatched her panties off the lampshade, wondering whether John had noticed them there the night before.

Water cascading down her body, her hands washed her lips, enjoying the ache of the torment that still lingered there from the night before. She teased her clitoris and then removed her hands away from temptation. Now was not the time. She needed to be thinking about her email to John, the one she was going to write that morning.

Finally dressed, she met John in the kitchen as he was finishing making the porridge and they carried it through to the lounge to watch the morning news together. Their connection from the night before was still very much alive, and they chatted as they ate their breakfast together.

When it was time to leave, she gave him a kiss.

'See you later,' she said gaily.

She left for the office at the same time she did every morning. Only this morning, when she was a block away, she phoned her office to call in sick and then made her way into town. Entering the local Starbucks, she ordered a coffee and took the table by the window. While she waited, she took out her laptop, fired it up, and connected to the free Wi-Fi. She opened her mail, selected "Compose" and sat back, her tummy doing little flips as she contemplated what to say.

The waitress brought her coffee over and Lisa looked at the screen over the top of the cup as she sipped it slowly. Two cups of coffee later, she had not written a word. How to start? What to say? She was stuck. Cross with herself, she decided just to start typing and clean it up afterwards.

Dear John,

NO, no no, this is not a Dear John letter. I am horrified at the things I said last night and the night before, well every night of late. I am so tense and tired and cranky from work when I get in, I cannot seem to shake it. Then you do something nice and that just sets me off. I know that sounds crazy, but that's what I feel like these days, a crazy person.

And this may be the craziest moment of it all, but I want to talk to you about Domestic Discipline.

I need your help to do better, to be better, mostly for myself, my sanity and happiness, but also for us, our relationship. I do so love you and want to get back to the 'us' we were when we first met.

I miss not feeling connected to you, close and safe and secure.

I have found this site with loads of information and a chat room with some great people in it, all talking about their relationships, many like ours and, through DD, found again that loving connection that had been lost along the way somewhere.

Why Domestic Discipline? Well, it recognises you as the leader of our relationship, a role you undertake so well and one I value so much. So that side of the DD we don't really need to address. I feel you step up, take charge, take care of the household needs and finances, decide what we will do and when to do it. Perhaps I have taken that a little for granted and sometimes, perhaps more of late, stepped on your toes and will take steps to appreciate and show my appreciation for your leadership going forward. Holding my hands up, I feel one of the major causes, if not the main cause, is my attitude of late. I have been taking out my irritations at work on you, attributing how I feel, the tiredness and frustrations of my job, to our relationship.

I am making myself unhappy, I am making you unhappy and I want to stop. I want you to help me to stop. From everything I have read so far and people that I have spoken with in the chat room, they suggest we should start with just a couple of rules which we should chat about and agree together, but I wanted to suggest some all the same.

Rule One. No foul language. I am a lady and must start to act more like one, which includes no swearing.

Rule Two. No snapping at you

Rule Three. No yelling, I can discuss disagreements without raising my voice.

Now, when you start reading about DD, you will quickly come across the fact that it includes punishments. Yes, I am asking you to punish me if I break any of our agreed-upon rules and YES, I am asking you to include SPANKING as one of those punishments.

Now, I have given THAT a LOT of thought, obviously, and asked a lot of questions. Why spanking? I think it's to do with being both physical and mental, a physical punishment to remember and learn the lesson, a mental punishment to ease the guilt and shame of my actions. Yes, I do feel those feelings, though I might not show it much. I also think the connection between you and me during the punishment is important too and feeling that even when I am at my worst, you still love and care for me enough to discipline me.

I might change my mind after my first spanking, of course, but I want to try.

I have taken the day off. Pulled a sickie, so will send this and then have another cup of coffee and await your reply.

Love you.
Lisa

Lisa pressed *send* and went and ordered another cup of coffee. She deliberately waited at the counter to stop herself from continually hitting the refresh button. As she waited, doubts assailed her. What if he thought she was crazy? What if he laughed at her, didn't take it seriously? What if he was not checking his emails? Should she wait here all day if necessary?

The waitress had to touch her arm to gain her attention. She handed Lisa her coffee and swiping the offered credit card in payment before returning it. Lisa took her coffee back to her seat and hit refresh on her laptop.

'YOU HAVE ONE UNREAD MAIL.'

Her heart pounded, her tummy fluttered with nerves. She clicked on the INBOX and saw it was from John.

She double clicked on the mail and opened it.

I like the idea; I will research. Come home NOW.

Love you too.
John.

Lisa sat back, excited and a little nervous. What had she begun? She finished her coffee and hurried home.

Entering her home, she found John on his laptop. He looked at his watch.

'Did you come straight home?' he asked quietly.

'Yes, of course. I finished my coffee and came straight back.'

'Go stand in the corner and consider your reply,' he said, pointing to where he wanted her to stand.

Lisa stood frozen; thoughts were whirling around in her mind. WHAT? WHY? Then her feet moved to the point John was pointing to. His arm had not dropped, his finger still pointing to the corner he wanted her to stand in.

STANDING IN THE CORNER, her mind shrieked. She had wanted this. Had asked for this, now it was happening. What was she feeling? She wanted to feel all those things she had read about, connection and security, but all she felt was confused, concerned. WHAT had she done? She played it over in her mind, *Come Home Now, did you come home immediately*? And she had, she had finished her coffee. . .. . . It clicked like the last piece of the puzzle falling into place. She hadn't left immediately; she had drunk her coffee to settle herself before heading home. She had disobeyed him. She felt a warm glow inside; she felt aroused; she felt chastised; this was so hot.

She stood facing the wall, wondering how long he was going to leave her for. The initial feelings had worn off. Now she was just looking at a wall, thinking; wow that could do with a fresh coat of paint. She knew she should not be thinking about that. She should be thinking about her disobedience and feeling naughty and ashamed, and she had for the first ten minutes or so she had stood there. Now it must be what, sixty minutes at least, she had been there so long. She had already created the shopping list in her head and was itching for a pen and paper to write it down.

'Ok, your ten minutes are up. You can come join me and tell me why you think I sent you to the corner.'

Ten minutes, TEN! It must have been longer than that. Hours clearly had passed while she had stood there. At least one, it felt like at least an hour. Ten minutes! Oh my god, what if that was his minimum time? What if he made her stand there for fifteen minutes or twenty?!

She walked over to John.

'It was because I did not leave immediately like you asked, but stayed to finish my coffee.'

'Exactly, I am pleased you worked that out for yourself. Talking of coffee, would you make us both a cup and we can chat about your email and what I have read so far?'

'Sure.'

Lisa practically skipped out of the room. His praise was like rain during a drought; she soaked it up and wanted more.

She took his coffee to him and sat on the sofa sipping hers, whilst he finished reading the article he had up on his screen.

'Ok, I have done some research and I will continue to do more and I would like you to do so as well. Chat rooms can be a great source too but watch out for the weirdos. I am not unfamiliar with the lifestyle concept, but would like to make sure you understand fully what we would be signing up to. The Agreement element I find valuable. This is not something I am imposing on you, but something we will consider and agree together.'

Lisa didn't trust herself to speak; this was going better than she had expected. She thought it would take weeks or months before John came around to the idea, if at all, yet he seemed to have taken to it immediately. This made her feel excited and a little nervous. So she just nodded.

'I reviewed your rules,' John continued, 'and agree with them. So that we are clear. Any and every example of coarse language, raised voice or snapping at me will result in a spanking. Is that the desire?'

Lisa nodded again.

'OK, agreed. We will keep it simple, with just hand spankings to start with and I would like you to have a safe word to begin with, Red for STOP and Orange which you can use if you need to catch your breath or change/adjust your position, things like that. Is that agreeable with you?'

Lisa swallowed and nodded. She could feel herself blushing furiously; her tummy was fluttering, but she also felt warm and peaceful. He was taking charge of her. It felt really nice.

'OK, I have a rule of my own I would like to include.'

Lisa's mind snapped into focus, a little weary now. So far, it had been her idea, her rules. Now he was introducing his own. Then Lisa chuckled out loud, which caused a look of surprise on John's face, which quickly turned to chagrin. Lisa held up her hands.

'I was taken aback that you had rules of your own, then found that funny as that is exactly what I am asking for,' she explained, a little hurriedly.

John laughed.

'Well, it is a good example of Be Careful What You Wish For. OK, my rule.

Remove all your pubic hair.'

'WHAT, FUCK OFF, NO WAY, WHY?'

Lisa slapped her hand over her mouth to stop herself from saying anything more.

DAMN, she needed to learn to control her mouth before shouting out the first thing that popped into her brain. Did he notice she swore? Did it count? Had they started yet? Her palms went clammy. She cleared her throat.

'Can you explain the reasoning behind that rule?'

There, that was better. Reasoned and quite ladylike.

'Sure.'

Oh, he sounds stern now, Lisa thought, rubbing her palms with her tissue.

'A, it will be a sign of your submission to me. B, it will act as a constant reminder we are within a Discipline agreement, C, it will denote your newness to the lifestyle, over time I will allow strips to be grown to reflect your growth in the lifestyle, eventually allowing a neat trimmed 'V' and D, because I would like it to be so.'

'Oh,' said Lisa, thinking furiously, all that sounded pretty good, she like the idea of gaining her stripes, so to speak, and she knew it would please John. He had mentioned it before and it would act as a constant reminder. It all sounded so reasonable she couldn't think of a reason why not, other than she found the idea embarrassing. But then again, she was asking him to spank her, and she knew that would be embarrassing too.

'OK,' was all she could think of saying. 'Agreed.'

CHAPTER SIX

Lisa left for work the following morning and as she made her way to the train station, she realised she felt happy. Going to work wasn't filling her with dread; the heavyweight in her chest was gone, replaced with a lightness of step that had her smiling.

Yesterday could not have gone better. John had taken to the idea with his usual zeal and was still researching, making notes, charts, and plans. After they had agreed their starting rules, John had informed her they would have lunch, then she would have an hour to bathe and shave, which had caused her to blush, following which she would get her spanking for the swear word she had used. Lisa had argued her corner, that they had not started their DD at the point, that it was only one word she had used, all falling on deaf ears which reduced her to plead she was not ready yet and could she not do corner time instead. John had been implacable, even quoting from the blogs he had read about the TiHs wanting their Head of House to be consistent and strict and not allow them to talk themselves out of a punishment, especially a spanking. So she resigned herself to her punishment, though secretly, inside she was pleased he had stood up to her and not back down from the spanking or the hair removal, although she was still in two minds about that one.

Later, sitting there, legs akimbo, cream slathered all over her bits, she thought; this is just like corner time, as she watched the clock tick oh so slowly down from the six minutes she had set. As before, six minutes seem so much longer, but John had been quite clear. She was not to allow the cream to stay on one second beyond the recommended time; there would be consequences if she had any burns afterwards. *It's funny how men react to women getting the slightest nick or graze*, she thought, remembering the time she had cut her legs shaving; he had been so concerned, then cross for her not taking more care. *They really think we are quite fragile.* She smiled. *That was not such a bad thing. Finally*, she thought as the clock "pinged." She stepped into the shower and washed away the cream and hair, feeling the smooth skin beneath. As her fingers slid over the soft surface, she felt tingles along her lips. *Wow, this felt amazing.* She explored herself, enjoying the absence of the usual rasping feel and sound from the rough wiry hair, now replaced by a silky smoothness which she preferred surprisingly. Drying herself off, she could not wait any longer and went through into the bedroom to stand before the full-length mirror. For the first time since she was a child, she could clearly see herself. She knew she had changed from the young girl to the woman; her inner lips had grown and she could clearly see them peeking out. She turned around and bent over at the waist, looking through her legs back towards the mirror and she blushed as now everything was clearly displayed. Both her intimate openings were visible.

This is what John will see, she thought.

She could not deny that along with the embarrassment of that thought came an arousal that surprised her. There was a second "Ping" from the clock and Lisa knew she only had ten minutes left of the allotted hour John had given her to "bath and shave." She quickly applied moisturising lotion to her body, again enjoying the smooth, soft feel of her now nude mound and lips before hastening downstairs.

Her brain would not simply allow her to obey John's instructions; it tormented her with comments;

'You are running down the stairs, naked, so John can inspect your pussy.'

'You are in a hurry, knowing you will be getting a spanking over his knee; you are a grown woman.'

'You are naked in the middle of the day.'

The funny thing was, whilst all thoughts were true, causing her to blush, not one thought suggested she should turn around and go back upstairs, and nothing seemed to stop her body from responding. Her nipples were rock hard under her touch, her lips were wet beneath her fingertips, and her stomach had that nervous flutter of anticipation and trepidation combined.

John took his time, running his hands over her body, his fingertips barely making contact, ghosting over the surface, causing goose bumps. Then suddenly, he was all strict and stern. He lectured her on just how bad her language had become, how foulmouthed she was and how unladylike he thought that was, how disappointed he was in her.

Lisa had taken it all stoically until that last bit; that he was disappointed in her. Unbidden, she felt tears prick her eyes. His opinion meant everything to her, a realisation that had just hit home.

By the time he had taken his seat and indicated that she should bend over his lap, she was eager to do so. To pay for her behaviour, to reset the counter so she could earn back his approval, banish his disappointment.

John wasted no more time and spanked her over and over. The smacks were not particularly hard, but they were constant, nonstop, and seemed to go on forever. At first Lisa was disappointed; these slaps were not going to give her redemption; they were not hard enough. They did not sting or hurt beyond a mild irritation. But as the seconds slowly ticked away, and his hand continued to rise and fall, she felt her bottom warm, and each smack stung just a little more. Suddenly it stopped, and she felt his hand stroke her bottom. Her cheeks stung a little, and they were warm beneath his hand.

'Ok, let's begin,' John said.

His hand fell again, and it took her breath away in surprise; it hurt. And the next and the next. Each smack on her cheeks stung like blazes and she squirmed as he continued on relentlessly. Accompanying the spanking, John was repeating how disappointed he was in her, how he would no longer tolerate coarse language and that even just one word would see her over his knee and getting a good spanking. As suddenly as it had started, it stopped, and she felt John's hand stroking her bottom. Her cheeks stung a lot now and felt hot under his hand. She wondered if it was over and felt a little deflated. He was still disappointed in her; he had said so.

Where was the forgiveness, she thought?

John spanked her bottom again, still firm, still relentlessly. SMACK, SMACK, SMACK, over and over. This time, John was telling her how he had faith in her; he knew she could do better, and he was proud of her for coming to him and asking him to help. How he would help her curb her language and was willing to spank her as many times as it took until she had it under control.

That last part managed to register a "*I bet you are*," in her head though it came out as

'OW, OW OW.'

The spanking got to the point of discomfort; it hurt, and she squirmed as she promised to do better. It took a second or two for Lisa to register that John had stopped spanking. His hand stroked her cheeks, which hurt and felt so hot. She let out a sigh of satisfaction. It was over and she had survived her first spanking.

SMACK, SMACK, SMACK. John started smacking her bottom again, catching Lisa by surprise... again! Her 'Nooo,' of displeasure was her only complaint; however, as she quickly realised, these spanks were not as hard as before. They stung her sensitive skin, but they felt forgiving, loving even, as they landed just under the curve of her bottom and the tops of her thighs. As he spanked her, he told her how much he loved her, how much he admired her for suggesting discipline to help improve their relationship and how he would work hard to be the man she needed him to be; to live up to those same rules, to set a good example. As her bottom got hotter and hotter, so her heart warmed to his words.

John told Lisa she could stand. He stood and hugged her; they kissed and cuddled. Lisa enjoyed the feel of his hands over her spanked bottom.

Lisa was dying to look though, to see her poor bottom spanked dark red, the pain to linger so she could wallow in the humbleness she felt.

When she looked at her bottom, she was quite disappointed. It was pink, yes, but not the raging crimson she had imagined whilst over his knee, and the sting was already fading. There could be no reproachful glances and bottom rubbing every time she knew he was looking. She was quite put out about that.

She enjoyed an evening of closeness as they sat together on the sofa, shoulder to shoulder. Every now and then, John would reach out and stroke her thigh or squeeze her hand. She even got a seat on the train. Life was good. She did feel a little robbed as she sat down; hoping for some twinge or protest, but her bottom gave no signs of the spanking she had received the day before. *Still*, she thought, hugging herself as a shiver fizzled through her body, *John said that spanking had been light for a punishment and that going forward there would be five sets of spankings not three and the fourth one would be with a wooden spatula.* He had shown her what he intended to use, the wooden spatula designed to push the material into the back and sides of the sofa.

She knew, without any doubt, that would hurt, but she was not afraid. She felt safe with John, secure in the knowledge he would not allow any harm to come to her, but would ensure her spankings were sufficiently firm to make them real and not play.

Work was work. She was a Project Manager, so always working to tight deadlines and milestones. Her boss was a tool who was riding her coattails, claiming her successes as being "under his guidance" which was one of her major stress factors. But today she felt quite light. She found herself smiling a lot and a colleague even commented on the fact she seemed happier today. The day flew by and at 6pm she got her coat and bag together ready to leave.

'Half Day?' her boss quipped.

Rather than take the bait, she just laughed and replied,

'Yep, it'll be half day, every day from now on. Night.'

And with that, she left with a huge feeling of satisfaction and pride. Usually she would have buckled, made some excuse why she had to leave after one hour of overtime instead of the usual three or four. In fact, she was taking a leaf out of one of the chats she had read online and decided she would leave work at 6pm each evening unless there was something urgent, and, should that arise, she would text her husband for permission to stay. If he said no, she would inform her manager of such and leave. She would make her boss's male chauvinistic ways work for her for a change. She was almost looking forward to such a time.

She made it home in good time, surprising John, who was working to her usual hours. Dinner was all prepared just needed to be popped into the oven, so she told John to continue his computer game and she would take care of dinner.

Popping the food into the oven and setting the heat; she had plenty of time for a shower and feeling "in the mood", she slipped on a small thin negligee with nothing underneath and headed back downstairs.

John's solider in the shoot-'em-up war simulator died about three seconds after she walked into the lounge. He didn't bother to revive him.

CHAPTER SEVEN

LISA - joined the chat.

Jack and Jill: I have had a tough but a good week DD wise.

Bambi: That sounds interesting, Jill.

Jack and Jill: At the beginning of the week I got into trouble for swearing, but last night I got busted for using my phone whilst driving.

Bambi: Is swearing one of your rules, Jill?

Jack and Jill: Yes, it was one of the rules I asked for. I can have a foul mouth at times and when my niece overheard me on the phone once and repeated the tirade in full, I was mortified. Especially when her mom asked where she had heard that. The kid pointed at me! I knew I had to control my words and asked Jack to have it as a rule to help me. It works too.... mostly.

Bambi: Oh wow, that's awesome ☺ How old was your niece at the time?

Jack and Jill: 5 😳

Bambi: Did you get spanked for that?

Jack and Jill: Yes, although it was not a rule at the time, I asked Jack for the punishment, too. I actually got two spankings, two corner times; one for the foul language and one for saying it in front of my niece. It was a lesson well learnt and my first experience of soap. YUK! Lol.

Bambi: Was texting and driving one of your own rules, too?

Jack and Jill: No, that was one of Jack's.

Bambi: And you said you were busted for breaking that one as well this week?

Jack and Jill: Yes, I texted him on my way home from work, and he suspected that I was driving so phoned me and when I answered he could hear the traffic and car so I was busted. He told me to hang up immediately, and we'd 'talk' about it when I got home.

Bambi: It is funny how all HoH's seem to use the word 'Talk' for 'punish.'

Jack and Jill: Lol. Well, once I got home there was not much talking I can tell you, plenty of scolding, though. I had to remove all my clothing 😳 and stand in the corner, hands on head. Once he had placed the 'spanking chair' in the middle of the room and positioned his paddle within hands reach, he called me over and I had to stand in front of him whilst he lectured me on the dangers of using my phone and driving.

Bambi: What's a spanking chair?

Jack and Jill: 🙂 Just one of the dining room chairs. I once made a remark that he always took the same chair from the table to spank me. From then on, it became the 'Spanking Chair'.

Bambi: Oh ok, I thought it was something you had ordered or built maybe 🙂

Go on with your story, if you don't mind sharing.

Jack and Jill: Lol I don't mind. It's good to share it with you guys. You understand and don't think I'm just weird. 🙂

Bambi: 🙂 😊 Not weird to us Jill, though we may all be weird together. 🙂

Jack and Jill: I have to admit I have heard it before but he got to me when he said he had been searching for me for years and now that he had me in his life he was not about to let me put myself at risk and lose me. It made it all seem so serious all of a sudden, and I was crying before I went over his lap.

Bambi: Awwww He loves you. 🙂 😊

Jack and Jill: He really does. Let me finish or you'll have me crying all over again. He spanked me first with his hand as a warm up, then got harder until I was kicking and feeling sorry for myself, then he picked up the paddle and whacked me with that whilst he told me off, all over again for putting myself and others at risk. He even spanked me whilst he told me he loved me.

I thought he could have saved that for the cuddle afterwards. ☺

Bambi: Does he normally spank you to tears?

Jack and Jill: No, mostly if I cry it's out of guilt for my behaviour or like last night, because Jack manages to say just the right sweet thing to make me feel so loved it made me cry.

Bambi: So really you were crying happy tears, all the while getting your bottom spanked. Lol.

Jack and Jill: Yes, I hadn't thought about it like that, but you are right. Even though I was getting a spanking that hurt, a lot! I was crying tears because I was happy and loved.

Jack and Jill: He was right to spank me too. It is a rule, it was selfish and irresponsible of me and I've leant my lesson. But that is not all; he took away my car privileges for a week.

Bambi: Oh no, don't you drive to work?

Jack and Jill: Yes and we have a rule that we both have to be home by 7pm or text why we are going to be late.

Bambi: Is that practical? Work has a way of throwing up all sorts of things that make leaving on time impossible.

Jack and Jill: I agree. We were both working so hard and both coming in at odd hours. We had no time together most evenings. Often we would eat alone and one or other would end up going to bed before the other. We sat down and agreed neither of us were happy. We agreed we would not work beyond 6pm, so no more than one hour's overtime unless absolutely necessary.

Bambi: And is that working?

Jack and Jill: Definitely, when it came down to it, there were few reasons to stay working late; often it was more out of drive and work ethic than a real need. There are few things that really cannot wait until the following day in our lines of work.

Bambi: And what's the punishment for coming home later than 7pm?

Jack and Jill: For me, a spanking.

LISA: And what about when Jack is late? I bet he doesn't get a spanking? It's that double standard that is challenging my thinking on DD.

Jack and Jill: Totally natural Lisa and very common. First, you have to remember we are asking or at least agreeing to the DD lifestyle; we agree the rules together. This could get me in trouble with the women's movement, but I think that a lot of women respond well to an authoritative figure and if not openly, secretly desire their man to take charge, assume a role of leadership in the family. Of course, each relationship is unique and the responsibilities vary wildly between couples but can still have that basic Leader/follower relationship.

Bambi: Exactly, with me and Steve. I look after the finances. I pay all the bills, see to our savings, and give Steve a weekly allowance. It used to be monthly but he would blow through it too quickly, so I manage his spending BUT he is still my Head of House and I follow his lead and accept his discipline. I wouldn't have it any other way now. Wish we had done it years ago.

Jack and Jill: Me too. Society today tells us we are supposed to be equals, more perhaps that women have to be better than men, but I don't feel less equal to my husband just because he is the Head of the House. I still have my say, my input and I am heard, perhaps more so than I felt I was before DD to be honest.

Bambi: Oh me too, communication is so much better than before. Now it's something we make time for. So you will have to use the train to get home for a week?

Jack and Jill: And a bus. I miss my car already just thinking about it.

Bambi: If you are home late because of transport issues, at least he won't spank you for that, Right?

Jack and Jill: No, we will. He made that point specifically. He carefully explained (it was quite funny actually) that he had thought about it and at first, thought the same as you; transport difficulties are out of my hands. But then he thought some more and the reason why I am on the train or bus in the first place was because I broke a rule, so he figures, it was my actions that starting the chain of events, 'the root cause' as he called it so it would result in a spanking. To be honest, I had just accepted his decision, but he had a chart and everything, some fish thingy.

Lisa: Fishbone Diagram, it's a way of drilling down to an actionable root cause of an issue.

Jack and Jill: Yes, that's sounds likes it. It looked like a fish. He was quite put out that I didn't require his entire thought process after all the work he had put into it.

Bambi: Awww, you should have let him, after all that effort.

Jack and Jill: You are kidding, Soooooo boring and besides he had a blast doing it. He enjoys that sort of thing. Total nerd.

Bambi: So after your spanking, did you cuddle afterwards?

Jack and Jill: Not right away no, I still had to do more corner time while he finished off making the dinner and I was not allowed to put on any clothing 😳

But after dinner, we had our cuddle. Three Times!! Lol 😳

Bambi: Oh wow ☺

LISA: Does a spanking always leave you... umm ready??? 😳

Jack and Jill: For me, it does yes. I think it has to do with Jack taking charge and showing his authority. The spankings hurt, and I learnt my lessons, but afterwards, all the heat seems to go to other places. 😳

Bambi: I too feel very aroused at the threat of a spanking, thinking about an impending spanking and when it's over. Well. . . I'm very receptive to his advances. 😳 😳

Bambi: I used to think there was something wrong with me. Who gets turned on by being spanked? Lol ME!!

Jack and Jill: When l approached my husband and explained l wanted this, his reaction was to say "how can the spanking be a punishment if you are aroused by it?"

Jack and Jill: It was a very difficult question to answer but l tried by saying it would be a punishment depending on intensity. Although, l admitted l would still be aroused, and that this was a natural reaction.

Jack and Jill: But also, when l receive a well deserved spanking it helps me clear the slate, and I feel forgiven, which also helps me forgive myself. 😊 And I have been feeling more randy since we started too.

Jack and Jill: For me, it's not about that though, although it is a nice bonus. For me, the punishment, the whole DD in fact, is about the closeness it brings between me and Jack.

I don't know if I can really explain it, but I feel renewed after a spanking, more than just forgiven, a feeling of inner peace.

Bambi: At the beginning, l earned a much deserved spanking and l asked him to spank me with his belt. He wouldn't, partly because he thought l wanted that. This is what led me to realise that a punishment spanking (even a hard one) would have helped me forgive myself and gave him an outlet for his displeasure at me. AND, had he spanked me, it would have helped the situation gain closure sooner. As it was, we talked the issue through (more of a long, stern lecture). But it took a while before I truly felt free of the guilt.

Bambi: It's been a long, slow process, and he now does spank me and he does get aroused himself by it. In fact, he is amazed and pleased at how eager to please him I am afterwards. 😊

Jack and Jill: I can get different feelings depending on why I have been spanked. If it's because I was feeling tense, that my life was somehow spiralling out of control, then a spanking reconnects me with my HoH, knowing he is in charge, calling me out on my crappy behaviour. Sounds counterintuitive, but having strict boundaries helps me with my anxieties.

Bambi: So you have been spanked Lisa, how long have you been in DD?

LISA: We have just started with DD and I got my first spanking for swearing last night.

Bambi: HUGS LISA, congratulations for starting your DD AND first spanking.

Goldie: Congrats LISA, your hubby wasted no time then?

LISA: No, as soon as I suggested it (I sent him an email) he started researching and reading all he could about the subject. He told me to come straight home (I pulled a sickie and was in a coffee shop), but I stayed and finished my coffee without thinking. He sent me to the corner for 10 minutes so I could think about it and figure out what I did wrong. Corner Time seems to have a time dimension of its own. I mean, 10 minutes seemed like forever.

Bambi: Lol, tell me about it.

Jack and Jill: Welcome to the TiH club LISA, so how was your first spanking?

LISA: Everything it needed to be in my opinion. I've been thinking it about it a lot. John spanked me in 3 sections not including the warm up. First was a light spanking, the second was the punishment, and the last was a sort of warm down. He told me afterwards that going forward there would be 5 sections, with the fourth being with a paddle but he thought the first one should be more of taster, nothing too scary, not too hard but sufficient to give me a good sense of what I am in for if I break a rule.

Bambi: That sounds good, LISA. Well considered, a warm up spanking is good as it will prevent bruising and I like the idea of a warm down. I have not heard anyone mention getting one of those before.

Jack and Jill: Have you ever asked for a spanking, Bambi?

Bambi: Oh gosh, yes. When I am feeling stressed, a good spanking is what I need.

Jack and Jill: Me too, though I might have been the only one. 😩 Though when Jack sees that I am stressed and does a 'preventative spanking' as he calls it; it makes it even more rewarding because he noticed.

Bambi: Oh my, yes. My Steve is getting better at recognising the signs, though at times he spanks me and says he 'thought' he saw the signs but has the telltale twinkle in his eye which gives him away. He just likes to spank sometimes.

LISA: Do you mind when you have been spanked and did nothing wrong or didn't need the stress relief?

Bambi: Not at all. I call it the 'just because' spanking and though I introduced it originally, he has adopted it wholeheartedly. ☺ Lol. There are times when I just want a spanking, for no particular rhyme or reason than just 'because' I figured out Steve feels the same way at times, but he usually claims it's for my benefit. lol.

Pat joins the chat.

Pat: Hi all, what are we talking about?

Bambi: Hi Pat, Jill was sharing her week of punishments, and we were talking about 'just because' spankings, and Lisa had her first spanking last night.

Pat: Congratulations Lisa. I don't think there's any better type of spanking than a 'just because' spanking. I go over his lap knowing he's not mad at me; I didn't misbehave, no guilt, no stress or feeling out of control, only that he wants or needs it for any number of reasons and I can just enjoy it. Well, a Good

Girl spanking is better; I take that back, but a 'just because spanking is a close second.

LISA: Bother, I have to go. But I will be back tomorrow. Thank you for sharing. Bye.

LISA left the chat.

CHAPTER EIGHT

A couple of weeks later.

Lisa started to unravel. They had so much to do before the party that evening; it was overwhelming her.

The day had started well. Both she and John had started the day with zeal; they had had breakfast and then headed to the grocery store for party supplies, and now they had pretty much cleaned the downstairs of the house between them.

John called a break for lunch, which is where Lisa started to come apart. The bathrooms needed doing upstairs. The bedrooms needed cleaning, the sheets changing. The kitchen would need cleaning once they had sorted out all the snacks for the night. She had to bathe, change and do her make-up; it was all too much.

As John prepared sandwiches for them both, he could see the signs of a panic attack in Lisa. He had done some reading and decided to try something new. Having read about stress relief spankings and how the other girls in the chat room talked about the benefits so he was willing, eager really, to give it a go.

He took Lisa by the hand and told her to follow him upstairs.

'We don't have time for this, John,' she complained.

'Hush. Trust me, we can take a few minutes, and if this works, you will feel a lot better. I promise.'

They went into the bedroom and John sat on the bed and shuffled himself so he was in the middle, his legs out straight in front of him.

'Jeans and panties off, Lisa and lay over my lap,' he said in a calm but firm voice.

It thrilled her when he used that voice. She obeyed without any thought of not doing so.

She went over his lap and felt his large hand resting on her bottom as he calmly explained that she was not in trouble; he was not cross with her in any way; that this spanking was going to help her de-stress and feel much better.

He spanked her with a steady but firm hand. Her bottom quickly warmed and stung.

At first she felt irritated; they didn't have time for this, and how a spanking could make her feel less tense was beyond her. She held herself stiffly; her mind crowded with all the things they had still to do. However, as the spanking continued, as her bottom turned red, her crowded mind filled with thoughts of the party and all those tasks still left undone were replaced by one single thought, that of her burning cheeks. The tension she had felt in her shoulders, the headache that had been lurking, eased and flowed away as the heat mounted and her bottom hurt. But it was a good hurt, a welcome pain, like when a masseuse worked on sore, tense muscles. She felt herself relax, her body now soft, draped over his lap; her head lay on the cool sheets as she gave herself up to her husband and his spanking hand.

This spanking was so unlike her other ones. Those had been punishments, where she felt bad, disappointed in herself and disappointing John, which was worse. Being scolded and spanked; she felt embarrassed bent over his knee, naked, bottom raised, exposed. This time, she felt none of that. She felt safe, loved, and cared for.

When he stopped spanking, John allowed her to lie there for a moment before giving her a hearty smack across her cheeks and told her to stop lazing around they had a party to prepare for. Lisa laughed and threw a pillow at him before scampering off to the bathroom.

John went downstairs and laid out the sandwiches he had made and poured the fresh coffee, spilling some over the counter as Lisa walked in stark naked.

'No point in getting dressed,' she said with a sexy smile and a twinkle in her eye.

John loved the change Domestic Discipline had brought to their marriage; he could not remember the last time Lisa had initiated anything sexy before and this was not the first time since they'd started either. He grinned and winked at her.

'Looks like that stress relief spanking did the trick, then?'

'Oh my, yes. I feel so much better. Light and energised. I can understand now what the girls meant in the chat rooms about inner peace and being a reset button.'

'Well, considering that worked well, if you behave for the rest of the day, we'll see if a Good Girl spanking stands up to its billing too,' John said, helping himself to a sandwich.

Lisa blushed and looked shyly at John.

John growled around a mouthful of bread, causing Lisa to laugh delightfully.

She, too, was enjoying this new side to their relationship; she felt closer to him than before and delighted in flirting and teasing him, like she had done when they had first met.

After lunch, they made quick work of the remaining chores. Lisa even enjoyed herself, making sure she was always bending over or reaching for something anytime John was in sight.

By the evening, all was done, and they enjoyed a shower together, something they had not done in years, as well as what they did *in* the shower together. They certainly were a lot closer than a month ago.

As she put the finishing touches to her makeup, she had a thought that made her smile and caused more tingles down below. She quickly put her plan into action as she heard their first guests arrive.

Making her way downstairs, she carried a secret smile, which certainly caught John's eye. When she saw he was looking at her, eyes slightly narrowed, she gave him a saucy wink and then laughed, greeting her friends warmly and ushering them through into the lounge.

The evening was going well; all their friends had arrived; the drink and food were plentiful and the conversation fun and light. Many complemented Lisa on such a fine spread, and her girlfriends commiserated on what a hard day it must have been for her, getting all this ready. Lisa smiled and laughed and thanked everyone for their comments, and would take John's hand and say she couldn't have done without his helping hand. She always felt her cheeks flush when she said it and she got many questions about the changes between John and herself. What had they done? What had they been up to for them to be so happy? One speculated they had won the lottery, another that they were expecting a baby; neither was true, of course. John and Lisa just laughed and said they were very happy and expected it to last for a very long time.

Half way through the evening, Lisa remembered her earlier plan, slipping out into the kitchen; she took out her phone and pressed SEND.

John felt his cell phone vibrate as he stood chatting with his friends about the upcoming soccer world cup. He took out his phone and pressed to read the incoming message. As the message slowly displayed on his screen, his heart beat faster and he felt a tightening in his trousers. He looked around the room, finding Lisa peeking over the shoulder of one of her girlfriends, trying not to look too gleeful. John smiled and waved, the phone still in his hand. Screen out; wiping the smile off Lisa's face as the message she had sent was a picture showing she was not wearing any panties that evening. John knew no one would have been able to focus on the screen in such a short time, but he felt it was only right Lisa felt a little mortification, as she caused him some embarrassment with his instant erection, though he wasn't cross really, quite the contrary.

The rest of the evening could not go fast enough for John. As he circled around the room, Lisa always managed to stay just ahead of him and always seemed to adjust her shoe or pick up her napkin, knowing John's eyes were firmly on the hem of her dress, watching it ride up, always just short of showing the curve of her bottom, driving him crazy with lust.

*

As Lisa shut the door on the last of their guests, she was surprised by John coming up behind her and taking her hands, placing them firmly against the closed door. She felt his hands glide over her body, cupping her breasts through the thin material of her dress before sliding lower. He pulled the hem of her dress up and tucked it into the thin belt she was wearing, exposing her bottom. He slid his left arm down to her bare legs and slowly glided it up and around until it was between her thighs, cupping her sex. She felt one finger slide without resistance into her opening, causing her to moan aloud. A moan echoed by John's growl as he found her so wet, so quickly. Lisa gave a small cry of disappointment as she felt his finger withdraw, then a louder one as they returned more forcibly, her tunnel opening and stretching around two fingers this time. John moved slightly to his left, his left hand dropping then returning with strength, his two fingers thrusting upwards inside of her, Lisa cried out again, but this time, not at the pleasure / pain his fingers brought but at the pain / pleasure his right hand elicited from her bottom as he brought it down across her cheeks with a loud SMAAAAACK. Both together, both hands in sync, his left, fingers thrusting up inside her hot wet passage, his palm grinding her clit beneath its rough surface as his right hand landed across her bottom in hard smacks. She felt his hot breath on her neck as he whispered hoarsely,

'You have been such a good girl,' SMAAAACCCK.

'What a delightfully naughty minx.' THRUSSSSST.

'Teasing me all day.' SMAACCCCK,

'I am so proud to have such an inventive and playful wife.'

THRUSSSSST,

'I am going to take my revenge on your bottom.'

SMAAACCCCK

'And then have my way with you.'

THRUSSSSST.

He bit her neck in response to his own arousal, his own desire making him deliciously, painfully, harder every time she cried out from a spank; and every time she moaned from a thrust, he let out his own growl that she loved to hear.

'I'm going to cum,' she whispered urgently, instinctively knowing he was not finished with her yet.

'No, you're not,' he said firmly. 'Not before I do.'

She felt her hair grabbed and pulled back, tilting her face towards his. Not violently, not abusively; but firmly, dominantly, pussy wettingly, perfectly. He kissed her hard on the lips and barely broke contact before he growled

'Upstairs NOW!'

She eagerly ran upstairs; her dress still tucked up into her belt, displaying her red bottom and red swollen lips to John's gaze.

John went around the house, locking doors, checking windows, necessary but really allowing his arousal to calm a little, to simmer below the boil, for another couple of moments and he would have spilled his load right there by the door.

He went upstairs, thoughts teasing his hardness. He found Lisa on the bed, kneeling on all fours, completely naked.

God, she looks *so* sexy.

He quickly undid his buckle and buttons on his trousers to release the pressure, as that alone would have fired him off for sure. He remembered the posts he had read and rolled up his sleeves as she watched him.

'All night you have been teasing me,' he said in his low, sexy voice. 'Now I am going to show you who is in charge around here.'

Lisa felt a shiver of anticipation ripple down her body; she felt the sexy throb between her thighs respond to each and every word.

'I am not a Head of House. I am *your* Head of House and I am going to give you a taste of my belt. Drop your shoulders and lift your bottom up, open those legs, show me what a good obedient girl you are.'

His words were like soft caresses on her lips, her pussy lips that is. Each one sending tingles along their inner surfaces. She knew she was open; she could feel the soft wafts of air as he paced up and down behind her. She blushed at the image she must be presenting and then pushed her bottom higher, her thighs a little wider, showing him her submission to his will, her display for his pleasure at the small cost of her own embarrassment. She heard the belt slide through the loops of his waistband and turned her head to look back at him. He held the belt in his hand, doubled over and looking innocent enough. Their eyes met, his questioning, hers asking. She gave a small imperceptible nod, and then buried her face into the pillows. She wanted to be able to cry out when the belt struck, to yell her pain and pleasure but knew her neighbours would soon be on the phone and the police kicking down the door as she gave full throat to her need, her desire to feel his power, his control and his love through the lash of the belt. She giggled into the pillow at the mental image of the police breaking in to find her presenting her bottom and John wielding his belt. Luckily, she had her face deep into the pillow so it did not break the hot erotic mood of the moment. Seconds later, she felt the first sharp sting of the belt, a wide swath of heat across both cheeks. It bloomed in intensity, reaching its zenith just as the second one landed. She let out a small cry into the pillow but kept her position so as not to alarm John. The second lash merged with the first whilst the third had just started to bloom.

How are the neighbours not hearing this? She thought as she cried out again into the pillow, a guttural sound of wanton lust, pleasure and pain.

Her bottom quickly grew hot, and the sting became a fire as the belt flew through the air and landed across her cheeks. She had lost count of how many lashes she had received; her bottom was a furnace of heat and pain. A lovingly desired, much needed, much wanted pain.

My god, how many ways were there to spank someone? She thought, as her bottom wriggled and clenched under the leather as it landed again.

She hadn't realised he had stopped, had not heard him ripping off his trousers, until a 'THUD' made her look up to see John struggling on the floor, one leg trapped around the ankle by his boxers and trouser leg.

She didn't have time to laugh or react as he kicked it free and seemingly flew as one moment later; he was inside her. She cried out as she felt his length sink into her depths.

Then he fucked her. She would like to have thought he made love to her, or took her or some other romantic notion, but "fucked" was the only word that described the pure animalistic nature of his power and desire. Her arousal, already simmering, fired up in response, but nothing was going to beat John from releasing his load that had built up steadily all through the day and into the evening. He exploded inside of her; she felt it erupt. Hot and wet, it filled her. She was happy, so happy that he had taken her for his own pleasure. No holding back or mind tricks to delay for her pleasure first, just pure unfettered erotic pleasure. His cry of pure ecstasy was music to her ears. She felt him slide out of her, but before she could move, his tongue was on her clitoris, causing her to cry out in pure pleasure of her own. She felt it swirl and slide over her hard bud before he sucked it into his mouth, giving her a pain / pleasure ache of its own. Then back to swirling his tongue as her orgasm, every bit as strong as his, tipped over the

71

edge and crashed through her body. As the first wave of her climax hit, her stomach muscles contracted, pulling her pussy up and in, breaking contact with John's lovely tongue. John was ready for that and immediately cupped her sex with his hand, his thumb sliding into her opening, his fingers sliding over her lips, trapping her clitoris beneath. She ground her pubis against his hand. She rode his thumb. She fucked him hard as her climax just kept on coming. She assumed later that she had had more than one, but at the time she was not aware of such details, just the need to buck and rub and fuck his hand.

Finally replete, she curled her legs into her body, squeezing them tightly together as John slid up beside her and held her, kissing her forehead, her eyelids, and the tip of her nose before she raised her head so he could kiss her on the lips. She felt his essence inside of her still, warm and gooey, slowly sliding out. She clenched her walls, her thighs tight, trying to keep his liquid love inside of her. For that was how she thought of it now, a physical representation of the love he had for her.

CHAPTER NINE

LISA: joined chat.

Maddy: I haven't been spanked in 4 weeks, which is a record for me, but I can feel the stress building up so that is not good.

sharon: that's a long time Maddy, a really long time.

Maddy: I told him tonight that I need a stress spanking and he told me . . . we will see. . . . ☹

Maddy: So I told him I will be the biggest brat ever if he doesn't give me what I ask for . . . MEN lol.

Jill: I was gonna say; time to get mouthy.

sharon: lol.

Linda: Just dump water over his head. That should get you spanked or some relief as you'll be laughing too hard to be stressed.

Jill: do it!!!!

claudia: We do stress relief as well.

Louise: When I do get stressed, if it's not taken care of promptly, I can spiral downwards pretty quickly.

claudia: I generally have to ask for them, but he's very accommodating in giving one if I need it.

Louise: How nice Claudia.

bambi: We do stress relief as well.

claudia: Yeah. . . it's always a tough decision though--you know how much you need it, but you also know how much it's going to hurt--I find them hard to ask for. ☺

Louise: Ditto and embarrassing yes?

claudia: I'm not really embarrassed to ask--I was embarrassed asking for DD to begin with, but asking for a spanking I need really doesn't embarrass me.

Louise: I nearly had a fit when he suddenly forgot. He had me waiting hours. Until he was like; Oh yeah.

claudia: Sometimes I'm a little afraid he might say "no."

73

LISA: I got my first stress relief spanking the other day. I didn't ask for it; my HoH saw everything was getting to me and just took me upstairs and spanked me.

Claudia: Did you feel better afterward?

LISA: So much better. I was much calmer and also energised, like I could take on anything.

bambi: I needed one of those. My emotions were completely out of whack most of the day today for no reason. Ugh lol.

Girl101: Oh bambi ☹ I'm sorry. I have those days.

Debs50: I'm like that often bambi it sucks.

bambi: I'm all good now. . . . .that was a whole other story. 😬

Girl101: I think I just get my feelings hurt easily. I need reassurance.

Debs50: He does that. Also, he makes sure he praises me a lot but punishes me as needed.

bambi: I'm the same way and Steve also gives me lots of praise when I'm doing well, which I really soak up like a sponge. ☺

bambi: Steve had a slightly clingy TiH on his hands today 😳 ugh I drive myself crazy when I get like that lol.

Girl101: It's okay to have a clingy day, Bambi. ☺

bambi: I know ☺ but I just get very. . . . .self conscious. . . . . . Not sure that's the right word, when I become extremely clingy.

Girl101: Like you're worried you're bothering or annoying him?

bambi: Yes. . 😳 I know deep down I'm not and he's reassured me every time that I'm not, but I get so stuck in my head at the time that I worry about that kinda thing.

Girl101: I used to feel that way too. Jon told me that was when he feels the most needed though, and that's a good feeling for them. They want to be needed by us.

sharon: I agree, that is what Iain said to me.

Girl101: Don't' worry about it Bambi 😊 it's normal. You aren't bothering him. You're showing him how much you really need and want him.

Steve: I wonder if it's the same for a woman.

sharon: It probably is Steve.

sharon: We all want to feel needed & wanted no matter what role or sex we are.

Girl101: Agreed.

Girl101: It's the same way that I like when Jon talks to me about his problems or work stuff. I like to feel needed even though he's worried to put his burden on me.

LISA: I had something like that the other day. I sent John a text, nothing important, just letting him know I would be home by 7pm and that I loved him.

Bambi: Aww that's sweet. Steve and I text each other every day, too.

LISA: Well, on this particular day I was like, 'why hasn't he replied yet' I kept looking at the phone even though it will beep, light up AND buzz to let me know a text message has arrived. So I sent him another text.

Girl101: Oh, Lisa, we have all been there. Text messages can be the worst when feeling vulnerable. It's the waiting.

LISA: I know. I could feel myself unravelling, turning into a crazy person even though I was telling myself he was probably just busy or hadn't noticed my messages.

LISA: Then I get a text saying 'Great see you when you get home 😊'

And I got teary. He hadn't said he loved me.

So I texted him back 'Don't you love me'

And waiting like hours for his reply.

Girl101: Did he reply?

LISA: Yes, he said he loved me more than ever. I was so happy I got teary over that, too. If it wasn't my time of the month, I'd think I was pregnant lol.

Girl101: DD does make us more vulnerable, Lisa; our feelings and emotions are much closer to the surface.

LISA: Yes, I think that's what I was going through with those texts. All part of the learning curve, I guess. ☺

OK got to dash. Only a short visit today, but I will be back. ☺

Girl101: Bye Lisa.

LISA: left chat.

CHAPTER TEN

The following month.

Lisa quickly slipped over John's lap, almost eagerly for their maintenance session.

The week was enjoyable, fun and exhausting, and not a little stressful. Five days ago, their family descended on them for their annual family week. Her Mom, dad, sister, her husband, and their two children, Sally, ten and Mickey, six, all arrived about the same time and since then it had been controlled chaos. Fortunately, her girls were still at University, so they had plenty of room.

She had been surprised when John reminded her that her maintenance spanking was due today. She had assumed he would wait until everyone had left in a few days before they resumed their DD. But she was grateful; she knew firsthand the benefits of a spanking when she was stressed, so whilst a little apprehensive about the pain from the spanking, she knew the effects would outlast that temporary discomfort.

So when everyone had said they were going for a walk before the big family dinner, John had winked at her, causing her to blush bright red. Which, of course, her Mom spotted and asked what was wrong why she was so flushed; she had even placed a hand on her forehead to see if she was running a temperature. Lisa laughed and said nothing was wrong and gave her Mom a hug in gratitude for her concern. It felt nice.

So packing everyone off, they had darted upstairs and now she was laying over John's lap, a mix of excitement and trepidation coursing through her. She felt her skirt flip up and the pressure of John's hand on her panty clad bottom. She gave a little shiver as tingles fizzed along her skin and a little moan as she felt his finger traced the bulge of her lips against the thin material, eagerly opening up her legs for more of that sort of attention. She felt the sting of a smack on her behind and heard the loud snap it made.

'Ohhh,' she thought and wiggled her bottom.

His hand rose and fell on her bottom, warming her up as he spanked her repeatedly.

Lisa allowed her muscles to go loose, her body just sinking onto his lap and the bedding on either side, simply submitting both in body and mind. She felt her bottom smarting under his hand.

He was taking his time this morning, enjoying each spank, allowing the heat of one spank to spread across her cheeks before landing the next one.

She found her mind slowly calm and let go of all the things she had to do, all the things waiting to be done and those that had fallen behind during the week of hosting her family. Soon her thoughts were all centred on her bottom and the heat that was steadily growing there. She could feel his "interest" in her spanking beneath her hip and she gave a little wiggle, letting out a small chuckle at John's hard smack response and a growled,

'Stay still.'

She felt his fingers slide into the waist band of her panties and she lifted her hips to help him slide the skimpy satin over her hips and down her legs, lifting each leg and bending her knee so he could remove them completely.

His hand soothed her spanked cheeks for a moment or two and Lisa practically purred within her contentment.

John's hand broke contact with her skin for just a moment, reconnecting as a smarting SMACK across her left cheek, followed by another SMACK across her right.

Now spanked Lisa in earnest. His hand rising and falling spanking her bottom, enjoying the softness of her skin beneath his hand and the slowly reddening blush spreading across her cheeks and the tops of her thighs.

Lisa felt the sting of her spanking all across her bottom and thighs. Nowhere seemed to have escaped his attentions. She picked up on his pattern, starting at the tops of her left thigh, up and over her left cheek, across to the right cheek and down to her right thigh before starting its return journey. Her bottom was now hot and stinging; all her thoughts were focused on her bottom, the heat; the sting of each smack, the trepidation of how much more was to come.

And there was more to come, a lot more.

John had a stressful week himself, playing host to his in-laws and sister-in-law. They were great people, but having a house full would always be stressful no matter who they were. So this spanking was as much allowing his stress to ease and dissipate as it was for her, not to mention a timely reminder that even with guests he was still in charge, still her Head of House.

Lisa's bottom was getting sore; her legs moved and kick; the fact she was revealing "all" in her mind, but not teasing her like it should. All her focus was on her spanking.

John spoke, reminding her he was her Head of House *all the time* and that she would do well to remember that. He pointed out a few examples where he felt she had forgotten that. His hand rising and falling, working over her bottom, ensuring the entire surface reddened evenly.

Lisa was wriggly and kicking from his spanks and the burning heat in her bottom. She promised to do better, apologised for her actions, even threw in a few 'Sirs' for good measure.

John was happy that the maintenance had done its work but wanted to spank out a little more of his own tensions, so he told Lisa he intended to do this.

Lisa was surprised when John shared he was feeling tense and wanted to spank her some more to work it out of his system. She gave her consent and stuck her head down and bottom up, feeling happy to help him, to ease his stress levels, although that didn't prevent her from letting out an 'Ouch, Ow, Ooow,' as each heavy hand landed across her bottom. She had tried to reach back to rub some of the sting away, but John just grabbed her arm, held it and growled that would cost her extra.

Such was her focus on her bottom and his falling hand; it took a moment or two for another sound to register.

'What are you doing?'

Lisa looked up from her position over John's lap, her bare bottom in the air and John's hand resting on her protesting cheeks to see her niece, Sally, standing there; her head tipped to one side in thought.

'We're just playing, Sally. Do you need anything?'

'Can I have a juice please?'

'Yes, of course, they're in the fridge; do you need me to get it for you?'

'No, I can do it.'

Sally turned and headed back downstairs.

Lisa sat up, her face beetroot red in embarrassment. John was also flushed as he helped Lisa off his lap and got off the bed, straightening his clothing.

Lisa scooted off the bed, looking around for her panties and finding them on the floor. She quickly stepped into them and looked at John. John looked at her, and then they both laughed. It started out just a chuckle, but as their embarrassment fuelled their humour, they were soon laughing so hard tears formed and Lisa was holding her sides as they started to ache.

As they went downstairs, it was not until Lisa perched herself on one of the high wooden chairs that her bottom reminded her she just had had a sound spanking and it brought a fresh flush of colour to her cheeks and a soft 'ow.'

John looked up, grinned and gave a wink, then with an air of innocent went into the lounge where Sally was sitting happily in front of the TV watching a movie, juice box in hand.

John and Lisa were pretty happy they had got away with being discovered. Sally made no further mention of it, her attention thoroughly occupied by the movie and then the games console, whilst they made the lunch.

Once everyone was back from their walk and washed up, John and Lisa laid out the lunch as they took their seats. Wine was poured; food dished out; everyone tucked in and silence reigned as they all ate. After a few minutes, they started some small talk, chatting about how wonderful the food was, how good the wine, how pleasant the walk had been. When the conversation turned to Sally and what she had been up to whilst they had been out, Lisa felt her tummy flip and she exchanged a quick look with John. Her sigh of relief was almost audible as Sally told them about the film she had seen in detail and then the games she had played afterwards.

Lisa and John smiled and turned towards Dad when he asked if they had had any free time for themselves that morning. Before they could answer, Sally, who was still enjoying the spotlight of the conversation, in total innocence, answered for them.

'Oh yes, they were upstairs; Uncle John was giving Aunty a spanking,' she announced before taking another bite of the roast potato stuck on the end of her fork.

She was startled when granddad and her dad spat their wine all over the table, and her mom was choking on her food.

Concerned, she quickly added,

'It's ok; Aunty hadn't been naughty; they were just playing.'

Lisa and John were beetroot red. As were both men as they coughed and spluttered, clearing their throats of the wine they had managed not to spray all over the table. Lisa's sister was looking on shocked. Only Lisa's mom had maintained her composure. She caught John's eye and gave him a conspiratorial wink and saluted him with her glass before taking a calm and controlled sip.

John gave an unconvincing laugh.

'Yes, it must have looked like that; I was giving her a massage.'

The folks around the table were happy to take anything at that point to allow the conversation to move on. Everyone but Sally, who was indignant about being told she had got it wrong.

'Na hah, I heard it,' she defended her position.

'Hush, Sally, that's enough,' said her Mom.

'But, Moooom,' Sally complained.

'HUSH,' she was firmly told.

Sally looked down, feeling hard done by, and shot a glare at Lisa across the table and John next to her, to make sure they knew she was unhappy with both of them.

'So where did you say you bought the wine?' asked Lisa's dad.

And the conversation, thankfully, moved on.

A little later, when Lisa was serving the pudding, she gave Sally a kiss on the head, ruffled her hair and an extra serving of ice cream after whispering,

'It'll be our secret.'

Sally beamed at Lisa, loving the idea of having a secret and an extra scoop of ice cream.

Lisa sat down, happier now that she had made friends again with her niece. She noticed her Mom looking over her the top of her wineglass, taking it all in and she blushed anew. Her mom just smiled, put her glass down, and tucked into her pudding.

CHAPTER ELEVEN

LISA joined the chat.

bambi: Welcome back Lisa. ☺

LISA: Thank you.

LISA: So I'm seriously starting to doubt my husband's capabilities in this DD thing.

bambi: Uh oh ☺ 😰 Lisa.

LISA: So he either forgot what he asked me to do today or he just doesn't care.

Erika: Did you do it?

LISA: I put away the linens, but forgot to clean up in the bedroom.

LISA: But I haven't heard a word about the other chore not being done, nor has he asked me about putting away the linen.

girl101: Is it possible he forgot, maybe?

LISA: He's always forgetting these days.

LISA: I feel like I'm constantly reminding him of his role, which is fricken pointless.

jen: Because we are new sometimes mine will let things slide until he realized that wasn't helping me.

LISA: And yes, while we are on the new side, he seems to be getting worse.

LISA: Lazy if you will.

LISA: You know the whole idea of "if you act submissive, he'll in turn become dominate."

LISA: It's a load of crap!

jen: How long have you been doing DD Lisa?

LISA: Jen, I'd say 2 months.

LISA: I feel a MAJOR bratting coming on, and I don't know if that will make or break this current situation. I've never bratted before.

LISA: I'm really not sure.

LISA: I've talked my head off, sorry.

sandra: If your HoH really wants this, he should make an effort (sorry, just cutting in, I was reading something else).

sandra: Honestly, my HoH is lazy - he says it himself. But he has a passion for the DD lifestyle and has seen how much it has helped our marriage.

sandra: Maybe you can just remind him how much it means to you for your relationship together.

girl101: Mine honestly doesn't have a lazy bone in his body, but he is not always consistent.

girl101: Have u talked to him about how this is making u feel?

LISA: Yes, and he has acknowledged that he needs to improve in this area.

LISA: It's like when he doesn't pay attention to these things, it's like a kick in the face. He's being totally self-centred.

girl101: I agree that a HoH cannot be a selfish person at all, really.

girl101: Lisa, maybe talk to him?

LISA: I will try to one more time. . . . but I don't know how to anymore without bringing him down. He has had such a poor-me attitude lately; I just want to smack him and say, "snap out of it!"

girl101: I am sorry, sweetie.

LISA: He's always saying I love you and I appreciate you, but never really seems to show it.

girl101: Tell him that, sweetie.

LISA: And if I just all of a sudden stop being the TiH I have been, I bet it wouldn't faze him at all.

LISA: Like I said, I will try one more time. It's not like I haven't before, it just doesn't seem to stick in his head.

girl101: I am sorry.

LISA: Me too.

LISA: Well, thanks for trying to help. Here is to hopefully falling asleep right away tonight and John coming to his senses.

girl101: Sweet dreams, sweetie.

LISA: Have a good night everyone.

bambi: Good night Lisa. ☺

CHAPTER TWELVE

That evening.

Lisa sat down on the sofa and stared at John. They had just had another argument, her fault totally; she was trying to shake him out of his DD lethargy. All that resulted in was a moody silence for an hour until John said;

'Let's talk.'

'Well?' she challenged?

'Well, what?' John responded, a little confused. He could feel his irritation rise.

'What do you mean, well what? We are supposed to be talking about our Domestic Discipline, which hasn't been happening of late.'

'Yes, ok.'

 John responded, looking a little guarded.

Lisa was losing her patience.

'So you want to stop doing DD, I take it?'

'No, I don't, I'm sorry. I enjoyed having DD in our relationship; I thought it was working for us and I kinda liked it. But perhaps we can talk about something else that would work just as well, something you would be happier with?'

Lisa was taken aback and more than a little confused.

'You liked us having DD?' she queried

'Yes.'

'And you think I didn't like it?'

'Yes.'

'Why?'

Lisa was totally perplexed; she could not think of anything she had said or done that would have given John the impression she was not happy with DD.

'Well, Matt said.... '

'Wait,' she interrupted, 'who's Matt?'

'Matt, from down the pub, Matt,' John replied.

'You told Matt about our DD?' Lisa exclaimed, her voice raising a notch.

'No, Matt was talking about this book.'

'What book?' interrupted Lisa.

John looked at her with that stern look of his; all steely eyed which, since starting DD, set her heart thumping, her stomach fluttering and a nice little tingle.

'If you keep interrupting, we'll restart right here, right now.' he growled.

Lisa bit back the first thought that came into her head; *Go on then, I dare you.* As much as she wanted to, she was also keen on getting to the bottom of John's recent lapse as Head of House, so she just nodded her understanding.

'Ok, where was I?'

'Matt, read a book,' Lisa prompted.

This earned her such a glare from John she held her hands up in supplication, her tummy flipping over in apprehension.

'Matt read that 50 shades book,' he continued. 'The one that everyone's reading, with the spanking and the caning and stuff.'

Lisa nodded to let him know she knew the book he was referring to.

'Well, he read about half to be honest, anyway He was saying this girl got a spanking, but she didn't really want it, in his opinion. She agreed to it for the guy's sake. She was all in tears and he was saying he wanted to spank her, so she followed his rules and behaved how he wanted her too. And he said that was out of order.'

Lisa put her hand up, stopping John mid flow. John felt the corners of his mouth tug, but he fought the urge to smile.

God, She looks sexy, sitting there with her hand up.

 'Yes?'

'He who?' Lisa asked.

'He who? Who? What?' John was confused.

'You said, "He said it was out of order." He, as in the bloke who spanked her or he, being Matt.'

John looked at her in exasperation.

'He, Matt, obviously Matt.'

'Not so obvious,' Lisa muttered under her breath.

'What?' John said with a hint of warning in his voice.

'Nothing,' she said, smiling sweetly with all innocence.

John growled his frustration. He was trying to maintain his sternness, but he never could resist that look of innocence she had perfected. All he wanted to do now was rip her clothes off. And Lisa knew it too.

'Go on,' she prompted

'Well, Matt was saying how wrong it was to make a girl think she needed to obey rules and be spanked for breaking them. How terrified she must feel all the time, fearful of breaking his rules, fearful of his punishments. He said he spanked her so hard she was in tears and still in tears hours afterwards.'

'OK, but that's in a book,' Lisa said, a glimmer of understanding forming in her mind.

'Yes, but Matt was right; it's not right to impose a set of rules on your wife, telling her how you expect her to behave and then punish her when she doesn't live up to my expectations,' emotion causing his voice to break.

Lisa moved closer to him on the sofa and took both his hands in his.

'Ok, now you listen to me. Did you bring DD to the relationship?'

Before John could answer.

'No, I did. Did you set the first few rules?'

Again, John opened his mouth to speak, but Lisa just talked right over him.

'No; I did. Now I want you to listen very carefully, John. This is important. I want this, I need this. I like the control you have over me. I want more of that, and I want you to punish me when I break one of *our* rules. Not your rules. I set most of them, and your rules. I agreed with them, so they are our rules too. I want you to set more rules and tell me how you want me to behave, even how to dress if the occasion arises and you have a wish that I wear something you like.'

John looked a little startled at Lisa's determination.

'OK,' was all he could think of saying.

'I mean it, John, and whilst we are on the subject, I need you to spank me a little longer than you have been. I want to feel really sorrowful for breaking a rule. At the moment I am learning the lesson ok but not really feeling remorse. I need that too.'

The tension seemed to flow out of John. He gathered her into his arms and held her tight.

'Spanking grounds me. I am very happy, calm and focused after a good spanking.' Lisa confided.

'You are like a whole different person after a spanking. I must admit that,' John said with a chuckle.

'Oh really? I was pretty sure I was an angel all the time!!'

John laughed, a real full bodied laugh.

Lisa didn't know whether to be indignant or laugh as well. Laughter won out, and they both laughed hard for a quite some time.

'I was reading this post about Boot Camp; I think we should do one,' suggested John.

'Oh?' Lisa replied, feeling her pulse quicken.

'Yes, I think it will get us back on track, reaffirm our rules, and re-establish our DD routine. I appreciate it's probably more for me than you; I would like to do it.'

Lisa was happy, giddily happy. He did take it seriously; he wanted to continue, and not just continue, but to work at making it better for him as well.

OK, she breathed excitedly. 'How does that work?'

'Well, it's individual, so I was thinking, daily maintenance, on-the-spot punishment spankings for every infraction and submissive tasks.' He replied, looking at her intently.

'OK, I am happy with that, except what are submissive tasks?'

'Well, tasks I set you, show your submissiveness to me by obeying without question.'

'Ummmm, ok, like what?' Lisa pushed, not sure about it.

'Well, if I ask you to go make me a cup of tea, you do so. If I tell you to stand in the corner, you do it. If I want you to spend the afternoon naked, you do so.'

Lisa's pulse raced a little again. She liked the sound of this more and more.

'I want you to take the week off next week so we can focus on it completely.'

Lisa was now sold.

'A whole week, lovely. I will book the time off tomorrow,' she agreed excitedly.

'Now, get the ping-pong paddle and we can take care of some of the spankings you missed.'

Lisa scooted off the sofa and ran upstairs to fetch it.

CHAPTER THIRTEEN

LISA: joined the chat.

Peter: Hi Lisa How's things? How's your HoH taken to DD? I recall you started about a month ago.

LISA: Find thanks. DD for 2 months now. We had a little communication breakdown but over all John has taken to it, perhaps a little too well. lol though I cannot complain about that too much, I suppose. ☺

Peter: Has he started to use implements yet?

LISA: Oh yes, the ping-pong paddle makes a regular appearance, and he has started to use his belt, too. Well, last night was the first time.

Peter: How is he with the paddle? Any good? Lol.

LISA: I never thought I would describe hubby as "good" with the ping-pong paddle when it comes to using it on me!! I will, however, admit that he is quite effective at bringing to my attention that I might just want to watch my mouth and rolling the eyes is not a good idea either. Sore backside, better attitude, grateful and happy today!!!

Peter: So, you had a spanking this morning?

LISA: Yes, before I went to work. Attitude seems to be his focus right now.

Peter: So you can still feel the spanking he gave you?

LISA: Lol oh yes!!!! Yes I do!!!
Now that it is over, I am glad he spanked me!!! During the spanking, I might not have had the same gratitude though. ☺

Peter: ☺ Its good there is a residual effect for a few hours, you can enjoy those effects, it's the getting them that is not so nice ☺ lol.

LISA: I love that he is actually willing and committed to spanking me as needed!!! I know the benefit for me is amazing and I cannot imagine that it does not benefit him to have a sweet, calm wife to deal with at least in the first few days after a spanking!! ☺

Peter: ☺ I am sure it does, and it's an inexhaustible supply of 'benefit' simply by re applying the spanking :) lol you could tattoo that on your Butt – 'Apply as needed' lol. ☺

LISA: Lol I am cracking up!!!

LISA: Now, I only want to be nice. . . . . ☺ But not too nice.

LISA: Spanking grounds me. I am very happy, calm and focused after a good spanking. He says I am like a whole different person. Lol.

LISA: I said 'oh really', I was pretty sure I was an angel all the time!! He really laughed. ;-)

Peter: Are you getting spanked a lot for attitude, then?

LISA: Yes ☺ it was a bit of "attitude adjustment" that took place this morning. Hubby now has a sweet, focused, energized wife to deal with instead of what he said was a mouthy, argumentative wife. He is quite accomplished at getting his message across using only his trusty ping-pong paddle Lol. I hate to admit that he was right, and this was just what I needed. ☺. It certainly was what I needed. It hurts like crazy but the effect it has is so worth it!!! I am grateful!!!

LISA: My last spanking before this morning was last evening; I thought that one would have been enough for me for a very long time. Guess I was wrong ☺ It was a total surprise. He told me to stand up, take my panties down, and bend over. He said I could hold on to the seat if I wanted to. I did what he said but. . . . . I said, 'I do not think I deserve this but will not argue as we made a deal that I would not argue or resist'. He said, 'you have had an attitude for 3 days and have needed this so I am going to help you out here.' I laughed and said oh thanks a lot. Lol. Bent over, in position and I hear him unbuckle and slide his belt off!!! Yikes!!! The belt???

Peter: How did the belt feel compared to the paddle?

LISA: The belt??? Hmmm, I am not sure how to explain that. Of course there is the initial sting but oh my, in about 3-5 seconds the BURN that follows is awful!!! When I said 'oh ow ow ow that hurts, it burns, oh please. . . . .' He said 'hush and get back in position.' I did. I thought it would never be over. I still told him 'thank you' when he was done. I must say, it was VERY effective. I think twice about my attitude in future and any smart remarks I might be thinking of saying. Lol.

Anyway, he finally got his message across; we proceeded, and I have had an amazing night!

Peter: so this morning was a reminder.

LISA: Not exactly. I slipped up a little and was a little disrespectful as I was getting out of bed, so I got a spanking this morning before I went to work.

Peter: But it's not all been smooth sailing since you started DD Lisa. You mentioned a slippage recently?

LISA: Yes, John had a wobble about the rights and wrongs of DD within a relationship, but once we actually sat down and talked it through, we sorted it out and we are picking it up again.

LISA: I was upset thinking he was not taking his HoH responsibilities seriously, like it was just a plaything, so I had a little attitude about that for a few days.

Peter: A 'little' attitude Lisa, really? Lol what caused the lapse, do you know?

LISA: Lol maybe not so little. It was a breakdown in communication. John thought I was only doing DD to appease him, to make him happy where it was me that wants and needs DD.

Peter: But you sorted it out ok?

LISA: oh yes, we had a talk and we are good now. He certainly made up for his lapse in my discipline. We are going to do a boot camp next week to really get going again.

Peter: Are you looking forward to that?

LISA: I can't wait. ☺ I have to go now. Talk later.

LISA left the chat.

CHAPTER FOURTEEN

The following week, Lisa and John started their Boot Camp.

'Go and shower,' John commanded, ushering Lisa out of the bed so he could enjoy a few minutes to himself. Once she returned, he ordered her to stand in the corner, hands on her head, whilst he quickly showered.

Lisa stood staring at the wall, a delicious anticipation coursing through her body.

When John returned, he ordered her to turn around, and her eyes were immediately drawn to just below his waist where his own anticipation was clearly evident.

'Come here.'

Lisa approached John, almost shyly; aware of her nakedness, her full nudity having removed all her pubic hair as agreed when they first started out with DD. John sat on the edge of the bed and guided her over his leg. She settled herself and waited for her first spanking of Boot Camp to start.

She had been expecting this; they had agreed she would receive a daily maintenance spanking each morning.

John started slow and steady, covering every inch of her bottom and down her thighs. Lower than usual, having decided he would try something new this week and spanked her down to just above the knee.

Lisa squirmed a little as the spanks landed on her thighs, stinging more than those on her bottom.

John ignored her mild protests and continued as he desired. This week Lisa was to submit to all his desires, whims, and needs, and he was looking forward to it immensely.

Not to say he was planning to take advantage of the situation. He had had a long conversation with Lisa, and she had made it very clear he was to dominate and enjoy this week, enjoy her submission and challenge her to be more submissive, to make her more submissive through punishment if she failed to obey. Ideally, they both hoped this would reset their DD and re balance their dominant and submissive levels to where Lisa desired them.

Her bottom and thighs seem to glow under his administrations, and Lisa certainly felt the heat and the sting of her spanked skin by the time John allowed her to get up.

As Lisa stood, her bottom seemed to blaze anew, and she hopped from one foot to the other, rubbing her bottom furiously as John looked on, amused.

After a few moments, John stood and indicated Lisa should kneel.

Lisa knew what was expected of her; indeed, she had been the one to suggest John incorporate this element into their dynamic. Oral was not something she was particularly fond of and oral to completion was something, until now, she had avoided. However, she felt submissive as she knelt before him, slowly taking his length into her mouth, swirling her tongue around the head. She used her hand to stroke his shaft, whilst she licked and sucked the top third of his penis. It didn't take long; thankfully, her jaw was already aching. She felt the telltale swell of the head and his hands softly on the back of her head grip her hair a little tighter, sending tingles of pleasure down her spine. Usually, this would be where she would remove his penis from the mouth and let him cum over her chest. This time, however, she curled her tongue backwards, just in time, as she felt the strong spurt of his cum against the underneath. Three, four strong spurts before it lessened. Once she was sure he had finished, showed by his chuckles as his cock became super sensitive, she pulled her head back and then swallowed the creamy liquid. It took her several attempts to get it all down, and she still felt it had left a coating in her mouth. She grimaced a little, not liking it one bit but feeling a little proud of herself for completing the submissive task.

John scooped her up in his arms and gave her a tight hug and then a hard kiss on her lips.

No tongue though, she thought, despite her opening her mouth in invitation.

No, all that earned her was a slap on her bottom and an instruction to go and clean her teeth.

When she returned to the room, she found John dressed and holding out a pair of her panties.

'Just these for now.'

Handing them to her, he headed downstairs.

'Time for breakfast, Lisa,' he called back up, fully expected her to make it.

She stepped into the openings of the panties and pulled them up, feeling the sting in her bottom had already subsided but not yet completely gone.

Blushing due to her lack of clothing, she hurried downstairs to make breakfast.

Breakfast was nice and relaxing. They watched one of their favourite shows they had recorded and had an enjoyable hour together.

Afterwards, John told Lisa to clear the breakfast dishes away whilst he nipped to the bathroom. Whether a moment of madness or a desire to test John's resolve, Lisa disobeyed and just sat there, so when John returned, the dishes remained exactly where they had been before he had left.

John looked thunderous.

'Are you not taking this seriously, Lisa? Do you not want DD after all?'

A terrible sinking feeling in her tummy made Lisa realised it had been a mistake to test him.

'Yes, yes, of course. I'll do it right away,' she said, scrambling up to clear the bowls and cups.

'LEAVE IT,' John said firmly. 'Get into the corner and get those panties off!'

Lisa quickly obeyed and found herself staring at the corner, fully nude.

After about five minutes, John ordered her over his knee.

Lisa turned to see John sitting on one of the dining chairs, meaning Lisa was going to be fully over his lap, staring at the carpet during her punishment. A position she found most embarrassing.

Once she was in position, John insisted she straighten her legs and open them wider so he could "enjoy the view," which caused further heat to rush to her face.

John changed up his normal punishment routine of three minutes of hand spankings, one more with the wooden paddle and a finishing warm down spanking with his hand. This time he alternated with the hand and the paddle after a lengthy warm up "to avoid bruising", he explained as his hand rose and fell across her bottom, "so early in the week", then the paddle which really stung. All the while, John was lecturing her about her commitment to their new lifestyle. This week was a restart, and he was not going to allow them to fall back to how they were before. DD was here to stay and if she didn't like it, she had better get used to it real fast. Even though the paddle was stinging her bottom a lot, his words were like fireworks going off in her mind, each one more amazing, colourful and wonderful as they exploded across the night's sky. Such a strong affirmation from John that discipline was here to stay was worth every stinging whack of his hand and paddle.

Once allowed to stand she danced on the spot rubbing her cheeks, heart as warm as her bottom and she practically threw herself into his arms, apologising for her behaviour, admitting she had been wrong to doubt his commitment, loved him so much and was very much in favour of DD too.

John returned her hugs with equal ardour and soon she was undoing his jeans and pushing them down.

Just as John entered her, Lisa grabbed his hips and held him still.

'You're not wearing anything,' she whispered.

'I know,' he whispered back. 'I thought we'd use this week together for more than just domestic discipline.'

Lisa let out a small cry of delight and pulled him down on top of her, legs wrapping around him just in case he had any thoughts of getting away.

"Baby dancing" was how one woman described it in chat, which Lisa remembered and made her chuckle as they went "at it" with abandon.

101

CHAPTER FIFTEEN

Lisa joined the chat.

Sweets: Hi Lisa.

Lisa: Hi sweets, I love your name.

Sweets: Thanks Lisa.

Sweets: I was iffy about using my real name, so I used the nickname S gave me.

Lisa: I figured there are enough people with my name that I would be ok lol.

Sweets: Fits me perfectly. I'm cute and adorable but can raise holy hell if I want to and then look so cute that it's really not fair to punish me *looks frantically for halo*.

Lisa: I love that.

Sweets: Me too, really, but still, I prefer anonymity online as much as possible.

Lisa: I understand.

Sweets: You new here, not sure if we've *met* before.

Lisa: I have only been on here recently so I still consider myself a newbie.

Sweets: Right. I've only been on here for about a month or so.

Lisa: Well, I am glad you found it.

Sweets: So am I, I have no one outside of here to discuss DD with apart from S so this is really fantastic for me.

Lisa: awww so new.

Sweets: For me and S we've been doing DD for about a month so far, properly that is, we were circling around the start zone for a couple of months prior to that though.

Sweets: DD is interesting, to say the least.

Sweets: We have our rules; I attempt to obey them with varying degrees of success. S enforces said rules and pulls me back in line if necessary.

Lisa: How is it structured for you?

Sweets: It is based around rules, but very rarely am I called out on them. Usually, the one I get in trouble for most is procrastination.

Sweets: But he doesn't refer to it as "You broke this rule, bad sweets!"

Lisa: that's the same for me, plus maintenance spankings now.

Sweets: It's more along the lines of "why did you not do what I asked?" and if I can't provide a reasonable explanation, I get punished.

Sweets: And we have maintenance spankings, which make up probably 90% of all the spankings I get, which isn't a lot to be fair.

Lisa: I am held to the rules very strictly, but they are very reasonable rules.

Sweets: I wish S was stricter, but he likes it how it is and he is calling me out on things a lot more now.

Sweets: Like last night, I bit his head off because I'd had a rotten end to the work night, and he gave me three opportunities to explain why I was in a grump and taking it out on him when I know I'm not allowed to do that, and then after five minutes when I'd remained silent, he towed me into the bedroom and spanked me.

Lisa: He never asks for explanations because he knows that in the case that there was a serious reason I broke a rule I would speak up.

Lisa: Like speeding to rush a kid to the hospital.

Lisa: If it's not a serious reason to break the rules, then there is no reason to break them, so I'm not even asked.

Sweets: Yes, S's reasonable like that too.

Lisa: Good for him.

Sweets: It's an improvement over the half hour it would have taken before, and even more of an improvement because he didn't ask if I needed it. He simply assumed I did and acted.

Sweets: It hurt too; he started off harder than normal and continued.

Sweets: And when I said something along the lines of "OW, OW, Ok, I get it, stop!" he didn't even pause.

Lisa: WOW good for him and you too.

Sweets: And said afterwards (because he always talks afterwards to ensure I got the lesson) he said that the reason he didn't stop was that I wasn't allowed to decide when I'd *got it* and therefore had enough, and apparently my tone was in direct contradiction to my words. ☺

Sweets: So he continued until he thought it had sunk in.

Lisa: That's great and the way I personally think it should be.

Sweets: It's rare for those "attention getters" to be needed, but occasionally I'll be really stressed out and can't actually ask for the stress relief spanking he'll cheerfully give me if I only ask.

Sweets: It's difficult for me to ask for a spanking on the best of days, even more so when I'm already wound up and pissed off

Lisa: I regularly ask for those since I know if I don't I could get one a lot worse.

Sweets: I try to, but some days everything just goes wrong.

Sweets: That's why I like maintenance. We do it on Saturdays and it sort of cleanses everything, and leaves me on a more even keel for the week.

Lisa: Mine is Friday night, so we can start fresh on the weekends, but we are doing a boot camp at the moment, so getting them twice daily this week.

Sweets: He doesn't like it when I take it out on him though, he's said on more than one occasion that there's a difference between venting about the horrible day you've had and snapping at the one you love just because you're in a shitty mood.

Lisa: Yep, I agree. That was pretty much how I was before we started DD; I was always taking out my frustrations on him. I hadn't realised just how close I was to pushing him away for good. DD saved me, saved us, from that.

Sweets: It's a form of disrespect, I suppose, and that's one of our rules, respect I mean, but again, he's never specifically called me out on any particular rule; he's just dealt with incidents as they arise.

Lisa: What is your view on submission and dominance in a relationship? Can either person do it or should it just be the guy or the girl?

Sweets: You mean whether the roles change or whether they should be concrete?

Lisa: Yes, are you of the "old-fashioned" viewpoint of that the woman should always be submissive to her husband or do you view it as it doesn't have to be that way?

Sweets: I don't really care. There are couples where it's the other way around and each relationship has to work according to the people involved.

Sweets: That said, I am a little uncomfortable around dominant women, mostly because I feel overwhelmed and intimidated by them.

Sweets: That's also true for alpha males as well, but I'm more comfortable around men than my own gender, if that makes sense?

Lisa: For me I'm most comfortable around; other submissive women, alpha men, dominant women, and beta men.

Lisa: In that order.

Sweets: And I'm certain that if the HoH's on here saw that they'd most likely be horrified, lol.

Lisa: About which thing?

Sweets: About me being uncomfortable around dominant individuals.

Lisa: ok.

Lisa: I'm like that too. I have no problem not being noticed and being in the back with other dominants in the room.

Lisa: It sort of happens here a lot with several HOH's in the chat room.

Sweets: Hehe, No, the HoH's in here are fine, mostly because we're all on computers. A couple in particular are lovely.

Sweets: But in real life, I'd have to almost be told they're friendly, you know, like dogs.

Sweets: If I see a big dog I won't approach unless told it was friendly, not because I'm afraid, I just don't know them.

Lisa: Haha, yeah I know what you mean.

Sweets: I tend to be very quiet when I don't know people; I'll sit back, listen, observe and then join in once I'm comfortable.

Sweets: Obviously I'll talk if people talk to me, but I usually won't initiate a conversation.

Lisa: I do not share the view of the woman staying at home and being a housewife and mom that supports her husband in whatever he does.

Sweets: Yes, my stepmother-in-law has that view, unfortunately.

Sweets: I don't mind being the cook, and the cleaner, and the general support, but I do want my own career too. S's always been fantastically supportive of me in everything.

Lisa: In my household, John stays at home and I work.

Sweets: I just take everyone on personality, but anyone who's really dominant; it's like my submissive nature wants me to shrink down and not be noticed. Don't know why, but it is.

Lisa: John loves not having a career, but he does some things for fun or to make some extra money.

Sweets: I need to run; I have dinner to make and an S to keep happy. Goodnight everyone.

Sweets left the chat.

Christine joined the chat.

Christine: Good morning or afternoon, perhaps. 🎁

Lisa: Just into the afternoon here ☺12:50PM

Lisa: Hi, how's you?

106

Christine: Been better but good lol u?

Lisa: Good thanks – 'been better?' Is that a reference to a punishment or are things not tip-top in your world at the moment?

Christine: Option A.

Lisa: Arrh, maintenance or infraction?

Christine: Both. ☹

Lisa: So Been Better refers to your posterior and good refers to your mental wellbeing?

Christine: Grounded from phone and doing things on my own for 2 weeks, no TV to top it off, daily reminders again.

Lisa: Oh my, was this all a result of the car ride the other night?

Christine: Partly and last nite I was so close to beating the last level and I didn't and my HoH was right there waiting for me to unload and I did.

Christine: Sometimes I don't think the meds help lol.

Lisa: I think that game is not helping, at all lol.

Christine: Nope, but it's ok now. I will have a two-week break or maybe that's how long it will take to fix my iphone, lmao.

Lisa: So going back to the 'I told you so' spanking ☺lol, I understand he spanked you on the off-ramp? So it was over the bonnet of the car?

Lisa: You threw the phone again?

Christine: Nope, slammed it very hard and yes about the car.

Lisa: What are you like? ☺

Christine: Naughty but nice. ☺

Christine: Short sweet most of the time usually not temperamental must b weather related.

Christine: What have you been up to?

LISA: We are doing a week long boot camp. It's going well though my bottom is permanently tender at the moment.

Christine: Oh sorry to hear that Lisa, I have not done a boot camp as of yet but I have heard they can be very beneficial.

LISA: It really is. John is taking to the dominant role really well and I am so proud of him. He is calling me out on all my shit and spanking me without hesitation when I deserve it.

And I sort of like the tender feeling on my bottom; it's like a constant reminder and I've been well behaved since I could feel it all the time.

Christine: ☺ That is so good to hear. Maybe one day my HoH and I will do a boot camp.

LISA: You should. They are worth it. Ok, better get going. I was only allowed 10 minutes chat before my nightly maintenance.

Christine: You get a maintenance each day Lisa?

LISA: Actually twice a day. We started out with just one, but I earned two punishment spankings on my first day! So John started maintenance twice a day but if needs be the second one becomes a joint maintenance and punishment.

Lisa: l would love to chat some more. Hope work is a quick and easy day for you.

Christine: Me too, we will see.

Christine: See u soon. 😬

Lisa: Ok bye for now.

CHAPTER SIXTEEN

Six Months later.

'So what's your secret?' Debbie asked, clearly distraught.

'Secret?' queried Lisa.

'Yes, what's the secret between you and John? We were sure you were heading for a divorce. I need to know. Gary and I are heading that way if we don't do something about it. We've been to counselling, but that doesn't seem to work and I'm about done.'

'I hadn't realised things had got that bad between you two,' said Lisa.

'I cannot remember when it was ever it was good,' grumbled Debbie.

'Do you argue a lot?' asked Lisa.

'We don't argue at all; that's half the problem. He's cold and remote. I can hear myself saying things, mean things, spiteful things, trying to get him to respond, to argue back and to care, but nothing.'

'He wasn't always like that though, right?'

'Truthfully, he has not changed much since we met. He's still kind and thoughtful. Placid is the word, I need more fire, more bite, I want him to be a man.'

'Putting him down and saying mean things is not the way to go though, Debs.'

'I know, I hear myself saying these things and I want to stop; I want him to stop me, but I just keep on opening my mouth and saying such terrible things. The other day we met up with a friend of his, taking him to dinner. When we picked him up, he suggested after the meal a couple of beers and then to watch a soccer program. Jake was all for it, and I can hear myself saying, *so now you are into football, being the big man now that Matt's in the car, never watched football before, now you're a fan.'*

Lisa was shocked.

'Seriously, Debbie, that was pretty rough, in front of his friend and all.'

'I know; I couldn't believe I was saying it, and it didn't stop there; it was awful; I was awful.' Debbie confessed, dabbing at her teary eyes.

'Last night was the worse; I was screaming at him; I lost it completely and I cannot even tell you why. I yelled and called him some horrible names. My language! I was using words I didn't even know I knew.'

'What happened?'

'He walked out; he left. I don't know where he's gone or if he is coming back.'

'Do you want him back?' Lisa asked, leaning forward.

'I do! I felt so alone last night, so miserable. I realised I still love him; I do, but maybe it's too late. Maybe I have blown it?'

Debbie looked at Lisa, desperate to be told she was wrong, that it was not too late.

'You can still save your marriage, Debbie. There is still time. I saved mine, well, John and I saved ours.'

'How, Lisa? What is your secret?'

Lisa sat back and took a sip of the wine she was holding and told her.

*

'He BEATS you!' Exclaimed Debbie. 'Seriously, that's your advice. Get Jake to *beat* me?!'

Lisa took a deep, calming breath.

'Not beat, Debbie, spank. There is a world of difference.'

'Not from where I am sitting,' scoffed Debbie, clearly unhappy with the solution at hand.

'I know it's a lot to take in, but you asked what my secret was and that's it, Domestic Discipline.'

'When John told you he wanted to spank you, what did you say? I'd have knocked Jake upside the head.'

'He didn't suggest it. I did,' replied Lisa.

'You suggested it! You suggested to John that he spanked you? This is all too much,' breathed Debbie, sitting back on the sofa, crossing her legs and taking a gulp of her wine.

After a moment or two, Debbie continued.

'So, let me get this straight. You asked John to spank you whenever you break a rule. But we are talking about a sexy, playful spanking, right?'

'No, we are talking full-on painful punishment,' informed Lisa.

'Ummm and who sets the rules, John?' Debbie queried, clearly trying to wrap her head about the concept.

'Nope, we agree with them together, but I suggested the rules about arguing, talking back, swearing, snapping, that sort of thing, and he agreed to those.'

'And has he spanked you?'

'Oh god yes, plenty of times. The first few weeks I was over his knee at least twice a day. It's not easy to break old habits, and that's what our troubles had become; habit. It was out of habit I would argue even when I was not really convinced by what I was saying. My "Go To" place was to swear and yell, rarely listening. My temper was just an "On/Off" switch. Rule Breakage spankings are less now but we have added maintenance spankings now.'

'What's maintenance?' asked Debbie, caught up in the conversation despite her aversion to the idea.

'Maintenance is a spanking, not as a result of breaking a rule; more to reinforce that there are rules to be obeyed.'

'This is crazy, so not only are you getting spanked by your husband, you are getting spanked even if you *don't* break the rules?!!' Debbie exclaimed incredulously.

Lisa smiled.

'I know, right? Sounds crazy. I know it does. What can I tell you? It works.'

'Sounds like some kinky sex fetish to me, and sex is the last thing on my mind at the moment.'

Lisa kept the fact that since starting DD, their sex life was better than ever. If Debbie tried DD, she would find that out for herself. She decided perhaps something visual would say more than words.

Standing up, Lisa turned her back towards Debbie and pulled down her sweatpants and panties to display her left cheek, where clearly, in a myriad of colours, mainly blacks and blues, was a wicked bruise of a handprint.

'Oh my god,' exclaimed Debbie, clearly shocked.

'Lisa, what are you thinking, letting him to that to you? I hope you gave him bloody what for!'

'Actually, I thanked him for spanking me and told him that if he had not spanked me good and hard as I deserved, I would have lost respect for him. Instead, I confessed I was impressed and slightly in awe that he followed through and gave me the spanking I needed.'

Debbie took another large gulp of her wine; trying to digest what she was hearing and seeing, thinking of which question to ask next.

'So you think this saved your marriage, then?' She finally asked.

'Definitely,' Lisa replied immediately. 'No question. It's not just saved our marriage; it's redefined it, created something better. John and I are closer than we have ever been, happier too. Communication is so much better, not just about this, but in all areas of our relationship.'

'You make it sound so wonderful.' Debbie said wistfully. 'I just cannot see this is for me, though.'

'Well, I can accept it's not for everyone. For me, it just clicked. When I started reading about it, I just felt something inside of me connect. I enjoy the chat room too as all the people are really friendly. Why not just take some time, read the articles on the site, perhaps visit the chat room and see how you feel about it then?'

Debbie sat quietly for a minute or two, accepting Lisa's offer to refill her wineglass. This was definitely a two or three glass conversation.

'Ok, let's go back a bit, these spankings; they must hurt right. That bruise must have taken some doing.'

'Oh, for sure, it hurts. It kind of needs to, to feel real, you know? The bruise; that was a result of John trying out a rapid spanking technique on the same spot that really stung but I was surprised to see the bruise to be honest. I think that might have been more to do with being spanked the night before as well, so my butt was already tender. I wouldn't say I like the bruise but I feel it means something. Like we are on a new journey and that he is really committed to this, and it definitely helps me behave.'

'I think that is part of what I am struggling with, having John tell you how to behave and punishing you when you don't.' Debbie confessed.

'Well, ok, in part that is true, but I asked him to do it, remember? I wanted, actually, I needed him to step up and take more control; not just of me but of the relationship, the household, take a more active role in making the decisions. Funny thing is; I didn't know that's what I needed until I read articles on the website and spoke to others in the chat room, and I felt that connection I mentioned earlier. I just knew I was unhappy and blamed John unfairly for that.'

Debbie digested that piece of information, comparing it with how she felt.

'Well, it was his fault then; he's the man he should have been taking charge and making the decision from the beginning.'

'Is that really fair, though?' Lisa challenged. 'Men today are raised with the idea that men and women are equal in everything. Be honest, do you defer to Jake? Do you follow his lead or do you bully, bribe, or sulk your way into getting what you want?'

'So you don't agree with women's lib, then?' Debbie retorted, feeling the sting of Lisa's last comment, as it was a little too close to home for her liking.

Lisa took a breath before replying, feeling her temper lift its head.

'Of course I believe in Women's Lib, so does John. But I choose to have John take the lead in our relationship; it feels right for me, for us. I am going to say more natural; it makes me feel very safe and taken care of. I don't want to be in charge; I want to have a say, my opinion to be heard; yes, but I do not want the final decision or even half of the final decision; I want John to take and own that.'

Debbie gave a laugh.

'Well, you just put the movement back fifty years.'

Lisa laughed too.

'Not so. The women's movement has given me the right to decide for myself and this is what I decided is best for me. I had to struggle with that idea since we started doing DD. That's why I was over his knee so often in the early weeks. John, though, took to it right away. He has grown since we introduced the concept of discipline; he is more confident, more assertive, and sexier too,' Lisa added, feeling her checks redden

'I knew it. Always sex with you,' Debbie teased.

'Oy, no it's not,' retorted Lisa, laughing.

'I don't want you to think it's all about sex; it really isn't, but an unforeseen bonus has been the massive improvement in our sex life. It's not just better; I want it more than ever too. John says I'm draining him.'

Lisa's cheeks were burning as she realised just how rude that sounded.

Debbie gave a throaty chuckle as she interrupted it in the rudest possible way.

'Dirty cow, Ok, so if it is not about the sex, what is it about?'

'Well, I have mentioned some of the key things already, *if* you have been listening.'

Debbie poked her tongue and waited for Lisa to continue.

'Ok, let me see if I can say this right. DD, for me, is about feeling safe and cared for. Setting boundaries without which I can feel like I am spiralling out of control. The physical element of the spanking can have many benefits. It eases tension and stress; it can be cathartic and guilt releasing; it can be sexy and very erotic. It can remind me to behave, to mind the rules before I break one and earn a punishment spanking. All of them, though, have one thing in common: I always feel peaceful and calm. Spankings are like an internal reset button, bringing me back to my good self. That combination of both the mental and physical has brought me closer to John, both physically and mentally.'

Lisa blushed again, shrugged and took a couple of sips of her wine as she regained her composure, a touch of emotion having built up as she expressed her thoughts aloud for the first time.

'Wow,' said Debbie, 'I'm lost for words.'

'I know, right,' Lisa said. 'Who knew spanking could do all that!'

'But if you like them so much, how are they a punishment?' pondered Debbie.

'Because they hurt,' Lisa replied ruefully. 'A punishment spanking is not like a maintenance spanking, for example. For punishment, you know you have broken a rule, let yourself down, and disappointed your partner. All those elements make the spanking a punishment. Those and the usually firmer application of the spanking implement; John likes using a wooden spatula. It's not just spanking, though. John has sent me to the corner a couple of times and sent me to bed once too,' Lisa explained.

Debbie threw her arms in the air, coming close to spilling what little wine she had left in her glass.

'Just when you've almost convinced me there might be something in this, you tell me more about how he treats you like a child!'

'I can see how that would look, yes,' conceded Lisa, 'and there is that element to it, I supposed, an embarrassment of having earned that punishment. But each time has been for my benefit. Both corner times were to let me calm down, collect myself and my thoughts, which were running away with me. The early bedtime, I hadn't been sleeping well for about a week and was dead tired, cranky and spoiling for a fight. Even though it was only 8pm and light outside, I was dead to the world the moment my head hit the pillow.'

'See; you keep making it seem reasonable, beneficial even, but I cannot help thinking you're making excuses for it,' Debbie said, exasperated.

Lisa felt calm, which surprised and pleased her. The more she had had to defend and explain her choice of having DD in her life, the more she had grown in confidence that, yes, this really was everything she was saying. She was not trying to sell DD to Debbie; it would be up to her whether she wanted to try it or not, but explaining it out loud had firmed up her own thoughts and banished those same negative connotations Debbie had challenged her with, once and for all.

'Not at all, Debs, I am only telling you my experience and how I feel about it. How you take it is up to you. If you want to save your marriage, this is just one possible solution. It worked for me, so much more than I thought it could or would. I cannot recommend it highly enough.'

Debbie looked thoughtful.

'Well, Jake won't go for it anyway,' she said dismissively.

Lisa let out a sigh.

'You will not save your marriage with that attitude. Take it one step at a time, do some reading, make your own mind up. If you think it's something you want to try, and then we can talk about Jake and how to raise it with him.'

'Makes sense,' conceded Debbie. 'I want to make my marriage work, and if I can get mine to be like yours, it will be worth a spanking or two.'

Feeling better for having a plan, Debbie held out her glass for more wine.

CHAPTER SEVENTEEN

LISA Joined the chat.

Catherine: Joined the chat.

LISA: How are you though? It sounds like you've had a rough few days?

Catherine: Yeah, I got in trouble, except this time it was for out and out being rude and disrespectful to Collin, which honestly is the first time I've done that since we started this.

LISA: Ouch. No need to tell me what happened next. I can guess.

LISA: And I thought I was in trouble over the other night. I got off lightly; it sounds like.

LISA: I read back over what you'd told others, and it sounds like you got a stern punishment.

Catherine: yeah, I know everyone is different in their punishments; it seems like mine is a lot but at the end of it, I'm okay.

LISA: Well, that's good at least.

LISA: And here I am complaining over four swats for ignoring my bedtime. lol. John has set a bedtime for me this week, Urrg!

Catherine: Collin will go tougher on me if I lied on top of something, and then snapping at him got me the worst I've had so far!

LISA: Well, that makes sense.

LISA: John doesn't like me lying to him either, but since it's only occurred twice so far, and both accidental, he's let me off with a few swats and a warning each time.

Catherine: yeah it makes sense. It's just a bit crazy when I reflect that we had absolutely no DD relationship six months ago to the extent we've gotten so far.

LISA: Snapping at him will earn me more, unless I heed his warning to mind my tone.

Catherine: What's the most you've gotten if you don't mind my asking?

LISA: Me, well, the worst I had has to be about a week ago, I think.

LISA: Both because of the argument which preceded it, the scolding (which was the most effective he'd ever given until then), and then the spanking, which was hand and paddle for around five minutes, with a threatened 10 min with a paddle if I didn't shape up!

LISA: I had an interesting thought the other night, though.

Catherine: I know, I guess I stupidly tested him. He's freaking consistent, so I'm literally pulling the tail of the tiger every single time. It's just still so fresh in my head.

LISA: It sounds like it.

Catherine: Was the 10 mins threatened or did he do it?

LISA: No, just threatened, because I haven't done anything to deserve it since then.

Catherine: What was your thought?

LISA: And the thought was that the reason I haven't got a harsher punishment is that I haven't done anything to deserve it.

LISA: So that led to the thought, well, what would cause that harsher punishment?

LISA: When I asked John, he said that he didn't know and didn't want to consider it, but if he had to guess, something like DUI.

Catherine: Right. Were you thinking you weren't getting it because he wasn't being consistent until you realized it was really just that you didn't deserve it?

LISA: I realised that I really didn't deserve a very harsh punishment usually, but I also thought that he might be holding back a bit out of fear of harming me.

Catherine: Yeah, that could be.

LISA: So I asked if he'd be willing to experiment a bit, and he said yes, we're doing it tomorrow.

Catherine: Good for you!

Catherine: No harm in testing it out

LISA: The experiment is for him to basically spank me at punishment level, until either I safe word or cry, one of the two.

LISA: And use different implements. Experiment with taking breaks during the spanking, basically testing how much I can take while showing him that it's not truly dangerous to give me a hard spanking.

LISA: And if he then decides to use the new level during punishment, well, I'll just have to be good. 😈

LISA: I like (sort of) where we're at the moment, but I'd like the severity scale to be measured on more than just different implements. I already know the wooden paddle and belt hurt, but I don't know how long he can spank me for before I truly can't take it anymore.

LISA: I mean, by the end of the punishments currently, I'm contrite, but the pain fades over a quick period. By an hour later I can sit pain free.

Catherine: I see, you know I've never safe worded, but in the beginning Collin said that he was going to go 10 minutes, and I thought okay I could handle that, a ten-minute break at work isn't long a ten-minute drive isn't long, but that first time he did ten minutes seemed to take forever! I tried telling him no more, stop and he kept asking do you want to use your safe word? You have 4 more minutes, and then you have 2 more minutes, etc. But when he was done, I looked around and was like; I made it!!!! I didn't think I could be pushed that far. I then broke into tears, but I think it was mostly out of shock. All in all, I really wasn't that sore.

LISA: And during the spanking, I'm trying to crawl off his lap (which never works) but while it hurts, I don't really get to the level of just submitting to it. I'm still not quite fighting it, but definitely squirming.

Catherine: It's hell to stay still.

LISA: So I think it's not quite going far enough, but I had to find a way to bring it up tactfully and the experiment was my solution.

Catherine: It sounds like a great solution! It's going to help him out a ton too, because he's going to feel more confident by knowing your true limits.

LISA: It is, but I'd like to see if I can actually get to the stage where I just submit to it. I don't know, but it might take longer than five minutes OTK to get there, and most likely harder too.

LISA: This is why I brought it up with John.

Catherine: You are a good communicator.

LISA: He was a little unsure this morning; I'd tickled him and his usual response is to pull me into a hug, before using said hold to swat me.

LISA: I was pulling away, whining "no" (while grinning at him), and he stopped, saying that if anyone saw through the window, they'd think something else was going on.

LISA: I then informed him that no one could see through the window without coming right up to it and that if he felt I needed to be disciplined, he should just do it, regardless of if I'd said no or not.

LISA: Then I tickled him again, (and swatted him), which produced the expected (and desired) response.

Catherine: LOL

LISA: The expected part was I got my butt smacked. The desired part was *how* he did it, no hesitation, etc.

Catherine: Good, no hesitation, and consistency is definitely nice!

LISA: It is nice, consist, etc.

LISA: I'm currently trying to encourage him to display dominance at any opportunity; I love it when he does, and he knows it, so he's doing it more often, and often in subtle ways that no one but us knows, but it's still nice.

Catherine: Definitely nice, and no one else, but you need to know anyway, just as long as you feel it and like it.

LISA: So tomorrow hopefully if I'm on here I'll need a pillow to sit on, or at least be permitted to rub afterwards. Usually I'm allowed to do so immediately. He's never forbidden it, but I understand why some HoH's won't allow it.

Catherine: Yes, I understand some don't. Collin usually lets me rub afterwards, thank goodness!

Catherine: Unfortunately, I couldn't bring a pillow to work today, so it was a bit uncomfortable for most of the day.

LISA: John's a believer in that once the punishment is over, comfort is allowed, he'll even rub my butt for me if I do my *big sad contrite Kitten eyes* at him.

Catherine: Haha.

LISA: Basically, looking at him sadly and saying, "It hurts. Can you make it feel better?"

LISA: Sometimes he'll say, "It's supposed to" or some variant on "Poor you" but usually he'll hug me (which is normal), and then either allow me to rub, or do it for me.

Catherine: ☺That's good! I'm thinking you are going to need a lot of that after your experiment tomorrow.

LISA: Yes, me too, but if it helps, then it will be worth the pain.

Catherine: Exactly!

LISA: This is also how I managed to stay up late last night, even after ignoring my bedtime on Thursday.

Catherine: By using your kitten eyes?

LISA: He didn't see the need to restrict my bedtime to either an earlier time or the agreed time, and as it was Friday, he allowed me to set what time I went to bed.

LISA: I'm going to request that he allow me to give feedback during it, as it will be for experimental purposes.

LISA: I don't think he'll have an issue with it.

Catherine: So you are going to be the one tomorrow saying when you've had too much?

LISA: Yes, the idea is for him to spank me at punishment level until I either safe word or cry. I have a feeling that the tears might come first.

Catherine: Is there an implement you haven't used before that you want to try out?

LISA: Yes, his belt. John always says it's awkward to use, but I want to have him try it again, anyway.

LISA: He usually folds it in half to use, therefore it's able to be used OTK but we haven't really tried other positions, we both like OTK.

Catherine: Collin wraps the belt around and around his hand until there is a smaller length left to use vs. folding it in half. I don't know if that's what others do, but that's how he does it.

LISA: OK. And is it used otk or are you in another position? J doesn't like it because he says it's awkward and he doesn't want to wrap it around me.

Catherine: Sometimes otk, but also bending over on the bed. He wraps it around and around the palm of his hand until he only has enough left hanging that is like a little longer than the width of my hips, I'd say.

LISA: lol. I'll ask John to try both ways, and maybe if I either bend over the bed or on hands and knees. OTK is the best for us though because we don't have a lot of room for him to stand next to me and swing things at my behind.

Catherine: I think the more he wraps it around his hand, the smaller length on it he has left. He is able to move it around more and not hit the same spot over and over, but sometimes when he leaves it longer, it tends to hit the same spots more easily.

Catherine: So it just depends on what his goal is for my punishment at that time.

LISA: Ok. Sounds like an idea to try. I'll probably be regretting this tomorrow but still. . . .

Catherine: Haha

LISA: It would give me a break from the damn paddle and provide a different sensation. I might dig out our ping-pong paddle as well; see if that can be used effectively during punishment.

LISA: It's light though, so I doubt it.

Catherine: I thought ping-pong paddle wouldn't be that bad, but I've seen others on chat say it is pretty bad. I don't know; we might have to try that out one day as well.

LISA: Ping-pong paddle can sting a fair bit; we haven't used it seriously yet so it might be something to try at least.

LISA: It's due to its rubbery covering, its thin wood, but the covering makes it sting more. Interestingly, one side stings more than the other, can't remember which though.

Catherine: There you go, so you are trying new implements and possibly a longer punishment time.

LISA: We have to learn where my limits are and this is the only way.

Catherine: Yeah, maybe, but you'd also be regretting it if you didn't know what you were missing, so to speak.

Catherine: It's really a wise way for people to figure out their limits.

LISA: Yes indeed. I have occasionally wondered if certain implements are as bad as they're made out to be, but (a) we have no money to buy them and (b) I'm not *that* adventurous.

Catherine: everyone has a different pain tolerance level too, so 5 minutes might be awful for one person and it can be a walk in the park for another. Same goes for different implements it seems; everyone has a different idea of what is the worst for them.

LISA: Yeah.

Catherine: Mine is actually the belt, but then again, we haven't used much else. Collin likes using stuff around the house.

LISA: I can tolerate five minutes if it's mostly hand. John does 4 minutes with hand and then 1 minute with a wooden paddle.

LISA: I'm not usually aware of time passing while in that position, it sort of shrinks to "OMG, please stoooooppp."

LISA: and it never does until he's satisfied.

Catherine: Hahaha for sure.

LISA: Yeah. I can go red pretty quick, which is another reason for the experiment, I suppose.

Catherine: Can you talk during your punishments? Like saying please stop.

Catherine: I mean, I know you have a safe word, but can you say other stuff?

LISA: I can talk, and usually it's more along the lines of pleading, saying sorry etc, none of which is listened to; I've never got to the point of safe wording yet, but he's told me that he expects me to use it if I need it. I have a feeling that anything else wouldn't be listened to but that would.

LISA: He normally talks through the spanking, and if I try to escape sometimes, he'll say "You can't escape" while pulling me back. Other times, he'll just pull me back and swat me harder.

Catherine: I've come to not say anything unless it's answering a question he's asked. I used to say "oh not there" but then he literally will focus in on where I told him not to go, so now I just shut it and act like every area is great! ☺

LISA: I have on a couple of occasions (including once after maintenance) let my mouth run away with me. That only earned me more painful minutes OTK lol.

Catherine: lol.

LISA: Yeah, that wasn't my brightest idea. Especially considering it was during the post-spanking 'has the lesson sunk in' talk.

LISA: Which he does to ensure that I haven't forgotten why I was being punished in the first place.

Catherine: Hmmm yeah, I'm seeing why that might not have been the best time to let your mouth run away with you.

LISA: Indeed.

LISA: Especially since his response was to put me right back over his knee and continue where he left off for another minute or two, and on a freshly spanked ass! That is not pleasant at all.

Catherine: Not at all.

Catherine: Well, it's rolling on 3 am here so I better jet and attempt to get some sleep again.

Catherine: Hopefully I can settle my mind this time.

LISA: Yeah, ok, see you later. It was nice chatting, and hopefully you can sleep. Good luck and good night.

LISA: left the chat.

CHAPTER EIGHTEEN

Lisa opened the door.

Debbie looked up, tears streaming down her cheeks.

'He wants to end it. Get a divorce and move on.'

Debbie started to cry in earnest, heart wrenching sobs. Lisa immediately pulled her into her arms and held her close as she cried.

After a few moments, Lisa was able to get Debbie to come inside. As they sat down on the sofa, Lisa's arms curled protectively around her friend as she cried.

John poked his head around the door, exchanged a look with Lisa, and silently backed out of the room. A moment later he returned with a bottle of wine and two large wineglasses and a glass of water.

Debbie looked up, blowing her nose and wiping her eyes. She gave a little laugh of embarrassment.

'Sorry, John, for spoiling your evening.'

'Don't be silly,' he said softly. 'You'll stay for dinner.'

With that, John left to take over in the kitchen.

Debbie just nodded, which gave Lisa a warm feeling inside, seeing John taking control with sensitivity and Debbie responding without even thinking. The exchange had allowed Debbie also to regain control, and she gratefully took the offered glass of wine.

Lisa took a gulp of her water before taking up the other wineglass.

Debbie looked quizzically at her.

'Water?'

'John's orders. He's decided that I need to drink more water so he brings me this humongous glass of water every so often and expects me to drink it all.'

'He's really taken to being in charge, then?' Debbie asked.

'Oh yes, he's very Head of Housey these days.' Lisa smiled. 'But tell me about Jake. What happened? Did you talk to him about DD?'

'We never had the chance. I have been reading up about it since we last spoke, what, six weeks ago now and feeling really good about it. A couple of women talked about connecting with DD like a light bulb going off in their heads. Well, my light bulb must be one of those low energy ones, as it took a little while before I really connected with the whole thing. I was trying to be more submissive to him, more obedient, but it was hard; him, not knowing what I was trying to do. I am not sure he even noticed,' Debbie added, a little bitterly.

Lisa nodded in agreement. 'I've been trying to do the same and I know it is not easy.'

'Well, things had improved. We were arguing less, and I was feeling more positive about the future.'

Debbie paused and took another sip of her wine.

'That all sounds good. What happened?' Lisa prompted.

'I lost my temper. Jake was just being all cold and aloof, and I was trying to be respectful and a good wife. I made dinner and served him and everything and got nothing back.'

'Oh, Debbie, I'm sorry. So you argued?'

Debbie nodded.

'After I dumped the dinner in his lap.'

Lisa placed her hand over her mouth in shock.

'What did he do?'

'Nothing,' replied Debbie, 'just sat there with that annoying bemused smile on his face. So I dumped my wine on his head and ran upstairs.'

'Oh, Debbie.'

There was a funny side to this, and a smile was tugging at the corners of Lisa's mouth, but Debbie had not told the whole story and she needed to get it out before she could deal with it.

'He shouted something like; "I've had enough of this shit," and then he left.'

Debbie sniffed and dabbed her eyes, taking another large sip of her wine.

'Wait, so he never said he wanted a divorce then?'

'Well, it's obvious, isn't it? He said he'd had enough,' countered Debbie, clearly hoping Lisa would disagree.

Lisa didn't disappoint.

'No, silly. Trust me, if he wanted a divorce, he would have said so. I am not saying everything is ok, but I am saying you have time to fix it and it's a great opening to discuss DD.'

Debbie looked a little happier, brighter.

'I could text him to say I'm sorry and want to talk.'

'Yes, that's a good idea, don't let him sit and stew on it,' agreed Lisa.

Debbie was already tapping away on her phone.

'Well, since he is wearing his stew, that horse has bolted,' she said and laughed.

Lisa let out a peel of laughter which just added fuel to Debbie's laugh and soon both girls were in fits of giggles. As one gained her composure, the other would laugh again, setting them both off.

'At least you washed it down with a nice glass of wine.'

And;

'Shouldn't have wasted it.'

Just set them off all over again.

John popped his head around the door, noticing the empty bottle of wine and two empty glasses, and announced that dinner was on the table, which set them off again.

Dinner was a bubbly affair. Debbie felt much better having texted Jake. She had told him she loved him so much and agreed that they had to do something. Adding, she thought she had found the solution and they should sit down tomorrow to talk. Jake had texted back saying he loved her too and wanted to fix their marriage. He followed to say he would be staying over at his mates' house as his clothes were in the washing machine.

When she shared this message with Lisa and John; Lisa, after an agreement nod from John, insisted Debbie stay the night, which she happily accepted, along with another glass of wine.

Debbie felt warm inside and not just because of the wine. She felt, for the first time in such a long time, an excitement about her relationship with Jake, anticipation of starting Domestic Discipline and seeing those wonderful benefits she had read time and time again. She even got to see it in action when Lisa went to top up their wineglasses.

John just said;

'I think you both have had enough.'

And Lisa just nodded and put the bottle down. Her cheeks were already flushed from the wine, but Debbie was sure they coloured up just a little from the mild rebuke.

The old Debbie would have chided John and took up the wine bottle herself, but having read so much and wanting the lifestyle herself, she found herself following Lisa's lead and putting aside her wine for the glass of water that had so far gone untouched.

She had felt a tingle at the calm authority in John's voice and couldn't wait to hear that same tone in Jake's.

They enjoyed a delightful meal. Both girls were a little tipsy from the wine, which made for a lot of laughs and jokes, all of which John enjoyed just as much.

Whilst Lisa showed Debbie to the guest bedroom, John tided away the plates and glasses, stacking the dishwasher to run through its cycles over night. All except one glass he found in the lounge, one nearly full glass of water.

Upstairs, Lisa was already in bed when John came up.

'What were you looking for?' Lisa queried, having heard John opening and closing draws and cupboards downstairs.

'This.' John replied, holding up a tube of Heat Gel.

Lisa's eyes went wide.

'Have you pulled a muscle?' she asked, almost hopefully.

'Nope, I also found this,' John said .

John held up the large glass of water he had given Lisa earlier that evening.

'Oh,' was all Lisa could think to say.

John placed both on the bedside table and went through into the attached bathroom to get ready for bed.

Coming back into the room, he ordered Lisa to take off her pyjamas and panties; which she did immediately, though not without some trepidation. She had been spanked many times since they started DD, but this would be her first "silent spanking", as it was called. She slid over John's lap as he sat on the bed, legs out in front of him.

John squeezed a line of the gel onto his fingertips and, thinking it was not enough, added another line before rubbing it into her left cheek. He covered the usual spanking area, including the crease just below the curve where her bottom meets her thighs and a little down the thigh. The gel spread better than he expected.

After repeating the same on her right cheek, he allowed her to put her panties back on and they slid down together under the covers to cuddle, both curious as to the effectiveness of her punishment.

Lisa let out a soft, 'Ooo. I can feel it getting hot,' she shared with John, thinking to herself, *this is no big deal, not as painful as a spanking.*

133

Within a few minutes, tears were pricking her eyes as the gel got super hot, super fast. She let out a hiss and squeezed John's hands really tight.

'Oh, that's hot, it stings.'

'Hot like a spanking?' asked John.

'Yes, a really long one. Oh wow, can I wash it off, please? It's too hot,' she pleaded.

John shook his head and whisper;

'No.'

Lisa let out a soft cry.

'Meany, this is way worse than a spanking. It's really hurting.'

Lisa pulled off her panties and threw off the covers to try to get some air across her bottom to cool it off some.

'I might have put too much on,' confessed John, 'but adding water just makes it get hotter.'

'Umm, yes I think I read that in chat sometime back. It seems to have levelled out now, still really hot and prickly but not getting hotter.'

After a few minutes, Lisa found the heat bearable, though she made a mental note to make sure she drank her water next time.

She gave John a kiss and was surprised when he returned it passionately. This was followed by a small squeal of delight as John slid down the bed. Lisa immediately turned over onto her back, wincing a little as the heat in her bottom flared as it rubbed against the sheets, opening herself as John's head slipped between her thighs and she felt the first touch of his tongue along the outer edge of her lips. She gave a soft sigh and wriggled her body a little to get more comfy as she laid back to enjoy her husband's attentions. She felt his tongue opening her lips, gliding along their sensitive inner surfaces to the soft wet pinkness below. His tongue was hard on her clitoris, swirling and flicking to drive her arousal up quickly before he lowered his head to seek her opening. Lisa loved this the most and pushed her hips up to meet his questing tongue, letting out an audible moan as she felt his tongue slide inside her.

Next door, Debbie had all but given up trying to tease her body into an orgasm when her ears heard the moan through the paper-thin walls.

That's my girl, she thought, as her fingers found themselves back between her thighs, her ears straining to hear more.

*

Debbie and Lisa had been friends since college and had shared a room both on campus and holidays, so were no strangers to hearing each other having sex.

*

Lisa did not disappoint; as her climax raced to heady heights. John's tongue doing delightfully wicked things, sometimes soft and swirly, often hard and thrusty. Every time she felt his tongue push inside her, seeking her depths, her arousal would jump another level and her moans of pleasure became louder.

Feeling Lisa's fingers sliding through his hair, John knew this was the sign of her impending orgasm, sliding his fingers away from holding her lips open to holding her thighs open as otherwise they would squeeze; crush might be a better word, the sides of his head.

He lifted and pushed her legs up and backwards, opening her up more to his teasing tongue, allowing it to plunge deeper inside her, sending her over the edge with a loud cry.

Next door, Debbie smiled in satisfaction, her own need having been seen to a moment or two earlier.

Lisa cuddled up against John, kissing him tenderly. Her hand slipped down between them, finding him hard against her palm. She stroked very slowly, teasing him. She knew he would be aroused, excited and most likely close to cumming. He enjoyed pleasuring her almost as much as she had enjoyed it. So she went slowly, changing the pressure of her grip from hard and tight, too soft and teasing. After a few minutes, she slid her hand lower and grasped his sack in her hand and squeezed, eliciting a soft moan of pleasure. She kissed him and grasped his shaft again. This time she pumped fast, causing him to gasp aloud.

'No cumming until I say,' Lisa said firmly.

John licked his lips and nodded, not trusting himself to speak as it would break his concentration and currently he was halfway through reciting the alphabet, backwards.

Lisa returned to the slow stroke, silently counting to twenty before giving ten really fast strokes, then back to the slow. She didn't bother to count all the time, using John's moans and gasps as her guide. When she had brought him too close, he would say something like,

'K, k, I'm close.'

And sometimes when he was REALLY close;

'Careful, careful.'

Which she loved the most and often could not resist a wicked extra stroke or two.

Every so often she would slide her hand down and squeeze his sack, finally getting the anguished moan she had been working for.

About time, she thought, feeling the muscles in her arm tiring and feeling achy.

She kissed John passionately and whispered;

'Now, no playing during the night and if you are a good boy, I'll play some more in the morning.'

John moaned with pleasure. He loved it when she played with him, and she knew it.

'OK,' he whispered back, kissing her again.

They lay face to face, holding hands under the covers, Lisa's bottom sticking out the side to cool it off as they drifted off to sleep.

CHAPTER NINETEEN

LISA: ☺ It's impressive. You are new to DD yet you seem so together with it all.

Tina: I think it's truly what I've wanted/needed for years. Most of it is comfortable, yet being totally submissive is elusive to me. I'm getting better, but it is hard. I've had so much control for so long. I need him to be the complete total alpha male type, more dominant, more demanding, higher expectations, etc.

LISA: It's always interesting, no mention of the pain of the spankings, it is always more about the HoH stepping up and taking charge, understandable and impressive.

Tina: Oh, they hurt, but it's not about that. It's like childbirth, really. Once it's over, the pain is forgotten and you'd do it all over again.

LISA: But the benefits live on beyond the spanking.

Tina: Definitely. I'm not as hot headed as I was, my attitude is evening out. I'm still not thrilled about chores and rarely do them like I know I should.

LISA: For me it was more about getting control of myself, changing my way of thinking, not taking out my bad moods on my husband, not bringing work irritations into our home, that sort of thing. Funny thing is, since starting DD I am less stressed in work, and much less irritable when coming home. I think I would like to work on being more submissive to John next. I put him through a lot of crap over the years and I would like to redress that by being a better wife, put him first for a change. He always puts me first, so it's only fair.

Sally joined the chat.

Sally: Hi, Tina.

Sally: Hi, Lisa.

Tina: How r you, Sally?

Sally: Doing okay. I am working on embracing my submissive side.

Sally: Which wasn't as hard as I thought it would be, if I don't question it or over think it.

LISA: I am trying so hard to find my submissive side. I'm not good at not over thinking though, I can't shut it all off very well.

Sally: I'm trying little things. Like making sure he has a hot lunch ready before he comes home, making him a plate instead of having him fix one himself.

Sally: Lol, he's appreciating the extra effort though.

Sally: It's not terribly hard. It's like good manners. You have to work at it a bit, but they're free ☺ and it's my way of thanking him for the little things he does for me. So it's a two-way street.

LISA: I want to do it more; I can tell right away how much it means to John when I do. The time it is the hardest is when schedules are hectic and things are stressful, then I just snap and let everything fall apart.

Tina: I agree I plan on having the house cleaned perfectly and a good meal in the Crockpot for him when he gets home. Oh and I cut the grass. Damn, I need a present or something.

Sally: Lol Tina. That you do. I think the hard part is not taking each other for granted, because I'll be honest as soon as he starts doing that. I pull back a little.

Sally: I'm learning not to force it. Start off by doing little things. That way, it doesn't seem so hard.

Sally: I made a small effort like the hot meal thing.

Sally: You know my hubby doesn't even see it as submissive? Just sees it as me doing something nice ☺ which works.

Jack and Jill joined the chat.

Victoria: Heyyy Jack and Jill.

Jack and Jill: Hey Victoria, how are you?

Victoria: Good good, and you?

Jack and Jill: I don't know yet. It's only 6:45 in the morning, too early.

Victoria: Lol, had your coffee yet?

Jack and Jill: Not yet. I don't drink coffee. I do my morning tea and I ran out! Not a good way to start.

Victoria: lol, I am a tea drinker too, though being English I supposed that is no surprise.

Jack and Jill: Yeah, not surprised at all lol.

Victoria: Am I remembering right? You had the dishes to do before last night.

Jack and Jill: That was Lisa.

Jack and Jill: I have teenagers. I don't do dishes lol.

Jack and Jill: The saddest day of my life will be when the last kid moves out and I have to do the kitchen and bathrooms again.

Victoria: So your DD must be quite a challenge to fit in around three boys, all teens?

Jack and Jill: Sometimes, the youngest is 10, the other 2 are 13 and 15, but we are making it work.

Victoria: That's good.

Jack and Jill: My kids are early risers so we get up early for morning maintenance and then sometimes I go back to sleep but I have them in bed by 9, 9:30pm so we have time then also

Victoria: Have ever tried a boot camp or submissive week?

Jack and Jill: We are doing that now.

Jack and Jill: That's why we are up early doing maintenance daily right now.

Victoria: Are you doing submission tasks? I have heard about these but have not seen many examples of what they might be.

Jack and Jill: A little bit. We are talking about doing more. We are still learning.

Jack and Jill: Like my husband says, I have been a force to be reckoned with for the last 16 years, so it takes time.

Victoria: Are you happy to share what you are doing now, thoughts going forward, or is it a little too personal?

Jack and Jill: Honestly, we are starting slow. He gives me some things that he wants done and I do them and dinner at 6pm. No yelling at kids or swearing, being respectful, that sort of thing.

Jack and Jill: Our sex life is better than it has ever been because I feel much closer than I ever have before.

Victoria: Yes, that certainly seems to be one of the major benefits.

Jack and Jill: Yes, it's been pretty amazing. He says I'm wearing him out. Lol.

Victoria: lol.

Jack and Jill: Yes and the earlier in a relationship you do it, the easier I think it would be.

Jack and Jill: I have always been a strong personality, so I need to take baby steps so it doesn't backfire, but it is definitely working.

Jack and Jill: We had some newbies in here earlier today. I was hoping they'd make it back this evening when there were more people.

Victoria: There's been lots of newbies the last few weeks. ☺

Jack and Jill: Sometimes I forget that I'm still fairly new to the room. It feels like I've been coming here for a long time.

Victoria: I understand that feeling it's hard to believe it'll be a yr next month yet it feels like much longer.

Jack and Jill: We're almost to 2 years with DD. It really flew by.

Victoria: oh wow, that's awesome. ☺

Jack and Jill: It seems like just yesterday that I was nervously waiting for Jack to read my email asking him to give it a try.

Victoria: I bet it does

Jack and Jill: I was so scared that he'd think I was crazy that I stayed in the shower until the water went cold. Even then, I took forever to dry off and come out.

Victoria: Awww

Jack and Jill: I probably would still be in there if it hadn't occurred to me that he was going to come in after me eventually, if only to make sure I was ok.

Jack and Jill: Thankfully, he took right to it.

Jack and Jill: Well, once he got past the initial fear of hurting me.

Victoria: I was surprised too how quickly Mike took to it too.

Jack and Jill: Sorry,, I'm going to have to go. The dogs are going crazy and I need to see why. I'll talk to you tomorrow.

Victoria: that's ok have a good night, 🙂 😊

LISA joined the chat.

Victoria: Hi Lisa.

LISA: Hi Victoria. I was just reading back, so Mike? Who's Mike? Last time we chatted you were single and seeking.

Victoria: 😊 We got chatting a few weeks ago in here.

LISA: That's great and you have already started DD?

Victoria: 😊 Yes. Crikey, I feel so shy all of a sudden lol.

LISA: lol. No need around me Victoria, heard it all, seen it all, done it all lol.

Victoria: Lol Mike and I sort of just clicked right away. I was telling him what I needed and how I thought it would help me and he offered to help by being my HoH.

LISA: So have you met up in person yet?

Victoria: No, we live in different countries, so it's an online thing at the moment.

LISA: That must be challenging?

Victoria: It can be. We started out just with emails. I would tell him of my day and any slippages to the rules we have agreed and he would set me a punishment. I self spank.

Now we are using Skype and it's so much better. He is actually there with me. He sets the punishments, tells me what to use, when to start and when to stop.

LISA: Yes, I can see that. My Husband and I have fooled around over Skype before, when he has been travelling so I know his presence definitely adds to the, em. . . proceedings.

Though that was before we discovered DD. Ummm we have not tried that over Skype. He does not travel as much as he used to.

Victoria: I definitely prefer it now that he is there with me, watching, directing and taking charge of my punishment directly.

LISA: I will watch your posts with interest Victoria; see how the budding relationship develops.

Victoria: Lol. Well, so far so good, but as you say, it's very new.

LISA: Bye for now, Victoria.

Victoria: Bye Lisa.

LISA: left the chat.

CHAPTER TWENTY

Two months later.

'Hi, Debs. Come on in,' invited John. 'Lisa's upstairs, running late as usual. She's just got out of the shower. She'll be down in a moment.'

Debs gave a laugh and a playful smack on his arm as she slid past.

'Daft, she's got nothing I have not seen a hundred times,' she said over her shoulder as she ran up the stairs.

Bursting into the room, she caught Lisa fully naked and just stepping into her panties. Lisa was surprised at the explosive entrance but unperturbed at being caught naked. They had been roommates at college, seen each other with boys, and even shared a boy once or twice. Every girl experiments in college and Debs was the girl she had experimented with, more than once! All these thoughts flashed through her head whilst she stood frozen.

'Are you going to put those on or keep flashing your kitty at me? Not that I'm complaining,' Debs added with a playful leer.

Lisa laughed and pulled up her scanty panties.

'Damn girl, was there a material shortage?' Debs teased.

'I know right, you would not believe how expensive these were, too.'

'Tell me about it, it seems the less there is, the more it costs!'

Debs stood close to Lisa; she cupped her breast and glided her thumb over the nipple which hardened beneath her touch. She laughed and removed her hand.

'Good to see I've still got it.'

Lisa laughed too, her face a little flushed.

'You always did have the special touch.'

Debs gave her a quick kiss that lingered slightly longer than necessary before stepping back, a little embarrassed.

Lisa was a little embarrassed too, not from the kiss or the touch, but from the tingle in her panties.

'So, how are things with Jake?' she asked, seeking to distract her thoughts from the kiss and the touch. She could see feel the warmth of Debbie's hand on her breast. She shook herself.

Really, she thought, *we are hardly going to get down to it here and now. What would John say?*

Then she thought about what John would say, which made her smile.

'Hey,' Debs broke into her thoughts, 'what are you smiling at?'

'Nothing,' Lisa said, feeling her face flush. She really wished it would stop doing that.

Debs looked at her suspiciously, but continued with what she was saying.

'Jake and I are practically living separate lives now. We even sleep separately.'

Lisa was shocked.

'Really, I had not realised things had got so bad between you two.'

'That's just it; they haven't, not since we went our separate ways. Now we are civil to one another, even friendly. It's more like how we used to be when we first met and I was dating what's his name from college still.'

'Ok, well, that sounds alright, but sleeping apart. How long has it been since you had sex?'

'With another person?' Debs replied with a saucy smile. 'That would be six months or more, I'd say. Jake and I sort of drifted apart physically.'

'Do you think you're going to separate? For good I mean?'

'I do, yes. It makes me sad to think that but I cannot see an alternative at the moment. I love Jake and I knew he loves me, but it's not enough. I need the dynamic to change between us and I cannot see that happening.'

'But you've not told him what you want that dynamic to be?'

'Right, I'd prefer it if he came to that conclusion himself.'

Lisa laughed.

'Whilst I know there are men who think about discipline and would love to spank their wives; there are very few who would tell their partners they intend to take them over their knee, pull their panties down and give them a good spanking, *and* expect a favourable outcome. I know we expect our men to be mind readers, but still, there are something's we have to lead them to, and this is definitely one of those things.'

Debs laughed too.

'You're probably right.'

Lisa could see she had planted a seed of thought with Debs and suddenly realised she had been standing there, just in her panties, all this time. She turned to fish out a bra from the draw.

'So you can stay the night?' She asked, adjusting her breasts within each cup before slipping on a blouse.

Debbie was a little disappointed to see Lisa getting dressed; she had been enjoying watching her breasts bounce and move as she spoke. Not to mention the itch in her panties that she would have loved to have scratched. Six months was a long time.

'I can. I checked with Jake and he has no plans so can watch the kids, so I am a free agent this night and plan to enjoy it.'

'Excellent. I thought we'd have dinner at Joey's and then go to the club from there.'

'Sounds like a plan,' agreed Debs.

'So, what do you think?' asked Lisa, showing off her outfit. She had chosen quite a tight blouse and a short skirt that flared ever so teasingly as she twisted her hips.

'Perfect,' Debs said approvingly, 'that'll have the men drooling.'

Lisa laughed, pleased by the comment but still gave a shocked reply.

'I am a happily married woman; I do not want men drooling, thank you very much.'

'Think of me and the free drinks then,' Deb's retorted as she turned towards the bedroom door to head downstairs.

Lisa gave her a swat across her bottom.

'You're married too, my girl, and don't you forget it.'

Debs let out a playful 'Ow' and stuck her tongue out before leading the way.

John came out of the lounge to see the girls off. Lisa could see the wheels turning behind his eyes as he looked both girls up and down, taking in their outfits, their make-up and the air of 'party girl' that Debs was giving off.

'OK, girls, have fun. Lisa, you know the rules,' he said.

Lisa gave him a warm kiss and hug and whispered;

'Yes, Sir,' in his ear and giving him a saucy smile.

*

The girls decided to pop into a bar first for a quick drink and, within minutes, were approached by a couple of young men on the prowl.

As usual, there was one cocky one and one wing man who just smiled. The cocky one indicated to the barman he desired service and asked the girls what they would like to drink. Ordering four light beers, he turned on the charm and delivered what he thought was his killer line;

'Do I look pale in the face? I've just had a rush of blood,' he quipped.

'Oh, please,' groaned Debbie. 'Is that the best you got?'

The chap looked a little injured.

'Clearly it was,' said Lisa, smiling.

They had their drink and some fun banter, but then the girls excused themselves, explaining they had a table booked, and no, they did not desire any further company.

Laughing and feeling the warm glow of desirability and light beer consumed pretty fast, they left the bar and headed for the restaurant.

After a fabulous meal, feeling bubbly and ready for fun, having shared a bottle of wine between them, they hit the club.

Within minutes, they were flirting with another couple of men, older this time. They ordered a bottle of champagne, clearly hoping to impress, and soon the four of them were on the dance floor. Both girls twisted and writhed, more to escape the wandering hands of their admirers than the dance moves they would normally be enjoying. They used the crowds on the dance floor to make their escape and slipped away.

After a quick visit to the ladies and the obligatory stash of the toilet roll behind the cistern, a trick they learned back in their youth to avoid the "drip dry" option left to them once the loo roll ran out. And it always ran out. They headed back out.

Back at the bar, they saw the two gentlemen had moved on to two, much younger, ladies who were clearly impressed with the champagne to mind the roving hands, or maybe they were enjoying those hands. Live and let live, they agreed. Debs looked around for the next likely pair to buy them a drink, but finding no takers, ordered two bottles of water.

$10 lighter, they took their water and made their way upstairs so they could chat a little without yelling at each other over the music. As they leaned close, they were both very aware of each other, the heat, the perfume, and they both felt a little giddy.

Lisa laughed her nervous tension away and leaned back to watch the dancers below.

As usual, there was always one with moves. Loud, exuberant moves that screamed;

"I love to dance, and don't care I can't."

Still, no one was getting injured, as they all gave him a wide berth.

They wandered around a bit, getting a bit bored. Lisa text John to say they would leave soon and would be home by 1am easy.

Then they bumped into a young, mixed crowd by the bar. Literally!

One of the young lads turned, holding two plastic cups of beer right into Lisa, soaking her blouse, turning it instantly see through. He was totally aghast and even tried to dry her off with the napkins the bartender gave him. As he rubbed her breasts, Lisa and Debs just stood there giving him the "Really, you're going there"; look. This was completely lost on the young man. Luckily, a couple of the girls from his party came to the rescue, taking the napkins off him, much to his chagrin, and sending him off to their table with a playful smack around the head.

They ushered both Lisa and Debs into the ladies, removing Lisa's blouse and tried to dry it as much as possible under the dryer. As girls will do, they were soon chatting and laughing, becoming instant friends. Once the blouse was as dry is it was going to get, Lisa put it back on and they all headed back to their table. The young man, Mark, was sent off to get more drinks as his penance, and soon they were all drinking and laughing. The two girls, Sue and Karen, introduced the boys as Mark, Steve, and Paul.

'So what line did he use this time?' asked Sue, with a nod of her head towards Mark.

'Actually he didn't, he just went with the pour beer over my blouse opener.'

'Talking of which.....'

Debs leaned over and placed a finger under Mark's chin and raised his eye level from Lisa's chest to her face.

'She's up here.'

Mark blushed and turned his head towards Debs, but within seconds, they all could see his eyes sliding back again.

'It's not surprising,' said Debs, nodding towards Lisa.

Lisa looked down, blushing herself as she could see her damp blouse was still practically transparent and her nipples were rock hard.

She gave a laugh.

'Oh well, let him look.'

Mark looked sheepish for a minute, and then a small smile crossed his lips.

'I'm happy to offer my shirt. Do you know what it is made of?'

Lisa shook her head, not seeing the line for what it was.

'Boyfriend material,' Mark delivered with aplomb and a wide grin.

This earned him a slap around the back of the head from Sue, which set off a round of laughter.

'I would have gone with how do you like your eggs in the morning? Fertilised?' Paul quipped, which earned him a slap from Karen.

'Hey,' said Paul, rubbing the back of his head. 'No hitting.'

More laughter followed. Lisa and Debs felt pretty chilled with this group, so stayed a while longer.

'Ok, lover boy,' Debs said, looking at Steve, 'what have you got?'

Steve held up his hands in surrender.

'I don't want my head slapped.'

'No slapping, I promise. In fact, if it's good enough, I'll even give you a kiss.'

'Debs!' Lisa exclaimed, shocked. 'You will do no such thing.'

Debs laughed.

'Relax, it's just a kiss.'

Steve looked around suspiciously, but everyone looked excited by the bet.

He thought for a moment and then gave Lisa his best puppy dog looks.

'If I followed you home, would you keep me?'

The boys all cried;

'Lame.'

And

'Pussy.'

Whilst the girls all went;

'Awwwwww, that's so cute.'

They then looked at Debs, who shrugged.

'A bet's a bet.'

She stood up, stepped over and slid onto Steve's lap, placing one hand behind his head she lent in slowly. Everyone was holding their breath as they watched.

Debs slowly licked her lips, parting them slightly before placing a soft, hot kiss on the top of his nose. With a laugh, she stood back up, pulled her skirt down her thighs, having risen a few inches, and returned to her seat. The others all let out little laughs as they finally took a breath and Steve looked like a lost puppy for real.

'Awww, Steve,' sympathised Karen, grabbing his head and planting a kiss firmly on his lips.

He froze for a moment and then softened into the kiss. If Karen had intended a quick peck, she certainly lingered. Parting slowly; their lips breaking contact long before their eyes did.

Sue gave a cough, breaking the spell for everyone. Karen gave an embarrassed laugh and sat back down. Steve looked startled and was bright red. The frequent looks they exchange throughout the rest of the night suggested the kiss was the start of something special.

The evening continued, and the drinks were plentiful and even when, "Last Orders", was yelled out from behind the bar; Lisa failed to register the time, she was pretty drunk.

Once the club closed and ushered out into the early hours of the morning, Lisa and Debs looked for a cab, but the streets were empty.

Their newfound friends insisted on driving them home so they all piled into their car, Lisa and Debs, sitting on the laps of two of the young men, much to their initial delight but eventual discomfort as they were jammed in and unable to "adjust" themselves as their enjoyment got the better of them.

Eventually they pulled up outside Lisa's house and they untangled themselves from the boys and exited the car in a somewhat lady like fashion.

Opening the front door, they could hear John on the phone.

'Everything is ok, they have just got back. I am really sorry to have troubled you, officer. I guess I panicked. Yes, I appreciate you extremely busy and apologise. Yes, Sir, I will, Sir.'

Placing the phone back into his cradle, he turned, a mix of relief and anger on his face. Relief won out, and he hurried to take Lisa into his arms, his voice gruff with emotion as he told her he had been so worried and he loved her and she had scared him and not to do that again. He hugged Debs as well and pulled back to look them both over to make sure they were both ok. He looked quizzically at Lisa's blouse. Debs, seeing the direction of his gaze, quickly explained that someone had spilt a beer over her earlier in the evening.

'Is that why it's buttoned up, wonky?' John inquired softly.

Debs looked at the blouse and can see it buttoned up incorrectly, leaving a gap which displayed her bra and ample bosom to the world.

'Oh, I had not noticed that,' Debbie said.

Lisa looked down but could not really see the problem.

John took a deep breath and told them both to go upstairs, get some sleep and that they would talk about it in the morning.

Both girls were grateful for the suggestion and in the five minutes it took John to follow them up, he found Lisa asleep on top of the bed fully clothed.

It took him another few minutes to get her clothes off and into bed and then went to check on Debs. She too was passed out on the bed, so he got her into the bed as well; placing the bin by the bedside in case she was sick. John returned to the bedroom but was too wired to sleep, so he sat in a chair and watched Lisa sleeping. Finally, as the tension left his body, he drifted off.

*

The following morning, Lisa woke and groaned. Her head pounded and her mouth felt disgusting. She staggered to the bathroom and took a swing of mouthwash for instant relief and then cleaned her teeth. The hot water of the shower slowly revived her, and she turned over the events of the previous evening. It had been a great night, and she had really enjoyed it. The only thing she felt guilty about was the fact she had text John to say she was practically on her way home then finally came through the door 4 hours after their agreed 1am curfew.

She knew she had a punishment coming. Its purpose, resolve the conflict between her and John.

It was difficult to explain, but she knew talking about the missing three hours would put them both on the defensive, an argument would ensue, words not meant said in the heat of the moment, her previous evening would be spoilt and she would have the lingering guilt that John had a point. The simplicity of a spanking resolved.., well, everything. John makes his point. It dispels her guilt, removes rather than papers over the crack in their relationship all such issues cause and they are stronger than before, not weaker. The rest of day would be warm and loving, not cold and distant.

Lisa smiled as the questions faded and her mind settled. She was even looking forward to it, bizarrely, graving that special intimate connection their spankings gave them both. She just hoped he would wait until much later when this thumping headache had passed.

She was joined at the table by Debbie, looking every bit as worse for wear as she felt. John had brewed a big pot of coffee and an enormous plate of toast. That was about all their stomachs could stand, and they ate in silence.

After they had eaten, they felt a little more like themselves and thought getting some fresh air would be a good idea.

Lisa carefully avoiding being alone with John whilst Debbie was there, as they got ready for their walk. She didn't want to talk about the night before; she wanted her spanking, but as the minutes passed, not talking about it just made it worse somehow and the guilt built and built. It was tearing her apart.

As they walked through the kitchen heading for the back door, John called to Lisa,

'When you come back, we will talk about last night and your punishment.'

Lisa went from feeling marginally human to mortified within a second. She glanced at Debbie, who was looking directly at her, clearly having heard every word. Lisa nodded her acknowledgement and went into the garden.

Debbie put her arm around her shoulders.

'So this is Domestic Discipline in action. How do you feel?'

Lisa considered her thoughts, trying to sort through the jumble.

She laughed.

'Honestly, my mind's a mess. Just before he said that i wanted him to say something, but when he said it I wanted the ground to open beneath my feet now...'

'Now?' asked Debbie.

'Now, I just want it. So much.'

She turned back, and with a skip in her step, headed for the kitchen.

As Lisa went back inside, seeking out John, she felt calm. This *was* what Domestic Discipline was all about. She had fucked up; there were no two ways to look at it, no different point of view. If the tables had been turned, she too would have been frantic with worry; she too would have phoned the police, the hospitals, anyone and everyone she could think of to call. She had put him through that with a moment of thoughtlessness. One text to say she would be later than planned and all the worry would not have been necessary. John may or may not have waited up, but he would not have been climbing the walls with worry. Taking the offer of a lift from a group of people she did not know, well, that would have earned her a spanking either way. John's a reasonable man. A simple phone call and he would have driven to the club to collect them both and praised her for making the call, but she just hadn't thought it through.

Without DD, there would have been arguments, yelling, screaming, moody silences, more yelling. Not just today, but many days. All of which would damage their relationship, tearing little holes that never quite heal, weakening the bond between them until eventually it tears apart. This was so much better, John would spank her, no doubt and it would hurt, for sure, and she was not looking forward to it happening but desperately needed it too so she could release the guilt, put it behind her, move on together. She knew it strengthened their bond, brought them closer together, more in tune, more in sync with each other. She also knew she would feel much better inside once it was over.

Entering the lounge, she saw John on one of the dining room chairs, placed within the centre of the room, waiting for her.

Debs squeezed behind her and jumped onto the sofa, tucking her knees under her chin. She hugged her legs, flushed with excitement.

Lisa felt another wave of heat wash through her and looked at John to see if he was going to send Debs away. John didn't move a muscle, did not make a sound, and just looked at Lisa expectantly. Then he held out his hand.

Lisa walked over, placed her hand in his and allowed him to guide her over his lap. She felt her skirt flip up over her bottom, her panties slide down her thighs and she just ducked her head and waited.

She did not feel any animosity towards Debbie for not leaving, for not given them the privacy she desired. John was Head of House; if he allowed her to stay, then she would accept it as part of her punishment.

The spanking started hard and pretty fast, taking her breath away. Along with each smack, John explained his thoughts and feelings. How he had appreciated her first text to say she would be home by 1am. How he had waited up and watched as the minutes passed, and then the hours without a word. How he had phoned her cell phone over and over and sent text after text. How he had phoned Debbie's cell and sent her text after text. No response, no word, no information. How he had feared the worse; images of accidents, rape and murder had tortured his mind for hours. Every word was punctuated with a firm smack and her bottom was blazing within minutes, but she welcomed every slap, every flare of heat and pain as his words lashed her soul. She wanted him to smack her bottom until his anguish was absolved, his fears and concerns and ultimately anger at her when she had waltzed in without a care in the world.

He continued with how he had phoned the hospitals, the police, their friends to see if anyone had any news and the spanking continued.

Lisa was unresisting, welcoming the pain, the punishment for her actions, how thoughtless she had been and she was vocal in her apologies that it would not happen again, she would never again be so thoughtless, tears freely falling, not from the pain of her spanking but the guilt and shame of her actions.

John's tone and message changed, now he told her how much he loved her, how much he respected her for bringing Domestic Discipline to their relationship, how he valued its resolutionary benefits, its absolutionary results, the togetherness and deep abiding love he felt for her as a result. The spanking continued.

For Lisa, these words were like a soothing balm to her soul, easing her guilt, calming her fears, enhancing the safety and security she felt from her marriage and partnership she shared with John, her lovely, lovely John. Though a small part teased her mind as resolutionary and absolutionary were such made-up words, it was like a soft light breeze blew, caressing her mind with warmth and love.

160

She had not realised the spanking had stopped. Her bottom continued to pulse and flare as if his hand was still striking. When John allowed her to stand, gravity took the weight of her cheeks and the pain rose even higher and she hopped and jumped around as she rubbed her bottom frantically, trying to put out the fire. She felt ablaze back there.

John looked stern and pointed to the wall where she meekly went, still rubbing her bottom.

She placed her toes against the wall and then leaned in until her nose was touching as well and breathed. She had been punished. She assumed there would be more to come and was not disappointed. John announced as she stood, nose and toes to the wall, that she had a nightly bedtime of 9pm for the next week, each preceded by a punishment spanking.

Lisa just nodded and stood quietly, facing the wall. Her mind was calm, settled. The restlessness to resolve her behaviour had gone. It was done with. Yes, she had punishments still to meet, but the matter was ended and she knew she and John would be ok. They would enjoy the rest of the weekend, laugh, tease and kiss and make up the fun way, too.

Debbie was unusually quiet. She had started out aroused at the thought of watching Lisa spanked but now she felt... "Jealous." That was the word for it. The spanking had been far harsher than she had ever imagined. Lisa's bottom was such a deep, deep red she wondered how she was not howling right now, but she felt jealous. The love John and Lisa felt for each other, that connection they had willingly demonstrated in their own unique way in front of her. She wanted that. She wondered what she was doing with her marriage, how had she thought being single would be better, more fun when all she had to do was tell him about Domestic Discipline, convince him to try it and not just to save her marriage but to get it back on track, improve it to something better than it ever had been.

Though perhaps Jack would not spank her quite so hard, she thought, *Better yet; best not give him a reason too.*

Thirty minutes later, Lisa was allowed to step away from the wall, pull up her panties and join John and Debs for some fresh coffee and something a little more filling than toast.

The very air seemed fresh and clean and soon they were all laughing at the various chat up lines they had heard the night before.

.

CHAPTER TWENTY ONE

NewGirlDebs: joined the chat.

NewGirlDebs: Hi all.

Peter: Hi Debs, welcome to the Domestic Discipline chat room.

NewGirlDebs: Domestic Discipline, like spankings, right?

Goldie: That would be it, but some use other forms of punishment.

NewGirlDebs: Like what other forms?

Peter: As you read more and hopefully visit here more you will see talk of Corner Time.

Peter: Lines and Essays.

Peter: Loss of Privileges.

Peter: Grounding, bed times and curfews.

NewGirlDebs: And all this is for the TiH while the HoH makes the decisions?

Peter: Yes.

Peter: DD is a partnership where both parties desire one to be in charge, to have the final say, ensure the other partner follows the agreed rules and behavioural expectations and punishes when they don't.

Peter: One of the core aspects I have read many times is the TiH DESIRES to be taken to task, to be called upon her temper, or smart mouth, cussing, she WANTS to be punished (which in the case of spanking will hurt) so that she feels remorseful and improves those behavioural traits.

Peter: So I was wondering if you feel those connections to DD (might be an unfair question so early in your reading/research).

NewGirlDebs: No, not an unfair question and to be honest, I think I do. I told my partner when we met that I was a brat and a handful. I push just to see if I can and I feel if I'm not stopped, it will end our relationship. I have always been like this, idk why. It's not that I really want to be like that. I think I want to be stopped. But I'm not sure about it all.

NewGirlDebs: And he likes to be in control but I push and he has got to the point where he is giving in all the time to save our relationship but I don't really want that and it is all just pushing me to act out more. Question is, how do I bring up DD in conversation?

Peter: That is the common dilemma of the person who first thinks of it. 99% of which seems to be the TiH bringing DD to their partner. Some do it with a sit down chat, others by letter or email, some print off articles and posts that connect with their thoughts and convey them.

Peter: It certainly sounds like you have a good idea of how you would like to improve your relationship and DD certainly is one way.

NewGirlDebs: Yea, but I'm not sure how I could possibly tell him I think I need to be taken in hand. I don't know how he will react and it seems weird to tell him to do it.

Goldie: Debs u sound like me, or how I used to be, how old r u if I may ask?

NewGirlDebs: I am 45 years old.

Goldie: Well, never too late. I was OLD when we started.

NewGirlDebs: How old?

Goldie: Oh sorry multitasking I am 49 now. I asked him for DD after 22 yrs of marriage.

Peter: Hey 49 is not OLD! I'm 48, so still young with boyish charm.

Goldie: I don't feel old actually, since starting this I feel so much younger than I have in many yrs.

NewGirlDebs: So u asked him? How? And how did he react?

Goldie: Well, I researched for 8-9 months, then long story short, I told him I had been looking into a different lifestyle and it could help us, then I emailed him. Honestly, I think it was a 20 page email of stuff I had copied & pasted. I didn't know it was that long until he told me because he was printing it at work LOL.

NewGirlDebs: So what did he say, Goldie?

Goldie: He read, then sent an email back saying interesting, then researched on his own for about 3 months, then we began.

Beth: I think it's great! If we have something that warrants a "punishment" come up, then once that happens it's over, done. There is no more worry or bad feelings, which can lead to disjointed communication or nasty words. Which was common with us before we started DD.

NewGirlDebs: Yea, I want our relationship like that. No nasty words. No more fighting.

Christine joined the chat.

JACK&JILL: Pink not your colour today, Christine. Are you feeling green? Lol.

Christine: Hi.

JACK&JILL: Hi.

Christine: Actually, my outfit is all pink today.

JACK&JILL: Lol.

Christine: I was thinking that if I wear pink on for my clothes, I won't have to wear pink on my butt.

JACK&JILL: Let me know how that works out.

Christine: Lol.

JACK&JILL: My butt's been wearing a lot of pink lately.

Christine: Mine too, that's why the pink outfit, I'm hoping for a change.

JACK&JILL: What have you been getting into trouble for?

Christine: Swearing and smashing my cell phone and just being disrespectful and arguing. You?

JACK&JILL: Attitude and yelling, two of my biggest issues.

Christine: And his biggest pet peeve is the word 'no' which is my favourite word.

JACK&JILL: Smashing your cell phone is never in your best interest.

Christine: I could have used that advice one week ago, JILL. Thank you.

JACK&JILL: Hahaahha, right!

Christine: Lol.

Christine: So it will be two weeks of nothing but every day reminders.

JACK&JILL: Yeah, we are doing daily maintenance and then my attitude has been keeping my nights busy also.

Christine: I think it has something to do with the weather.

Christine: LOL.

JACK&JILL: Idk it's got to be something. Can't be me.

JACK&JILL: Because I'm perfect!

Christine: Right lol.

Christine: Ok gtg back to work, see u later.

JACK&JILL: Bye. Have a good day.

Victoria: Bye Christine.

JACK&JILL Hello Victoria didn't see you there.

Victoria: Hi Jill, just following the conversations ☺ Sitting a little tenderly myself today.

JACK&JILL Lol have you been naughty as well, Victoria?

Victoria: Yeh, I broke one of our rules, big time.

JACK&JILL Oohhh which one? If you don't mind me asking?

Victoria: I don't mind at all. I have a rule about having three meals a day and I skipped two of them lol.

JACK&JILL: Oh Victoria that is not good, you need to eat.

166

Victoria: Yes I know but sometimes I just don't feel like eating but then I get low on sugar level, get irritable and end up arguing with my sister. I have a rule about that too.

JACK&JILL: How does the discipline work for you Victoria, being in a wheelchair? Say if I am being too nosey.

Victoria: No, that is fine; I love this room and being able to chat with like-minded folk. I Skype with Mike and I have to tell him if I have broken any rules since we last spoke. Since I asked Mike to help with my eating and arguing with my sister, I can hardly hide the fact when I break the rules. There'd be no point in doing DD if that were the case and I really value DD in my life right now. It centres me, and gives me structure.

JACK&JILL: So how does he punish you?

Victoria: I have to transfer out of my chair onto the bed. Remove my pants and panties. Place the pillows in the middle of the bed and bend over them. Mike will then tell to start spanking my left cheek with my hand and I continue that until he tells me to switch sides and then eventually to stop.

JACK&JILL: Is it just hand spankings Victoria?

Victoria: When we first started, he used the hand and hair brush only and would email me how many swats I was going to get.

Victoria: When we moved to Skype he started to use other implements like the wooden spoon and spatula then it was my bright idea one day when I was "crazy bored" to look around the house for new implements and I found the dreaded bath brush and a plastic ruler *blushing*.

JACK&JILL: Lol, I did something similar. Jack used to use his hand and belt until I went out and bought a large wooded hairbrush. Wow, that thing stings and after a few seconds my bottom has a deeper heat to it. Trust me, after a spanking with the brush, I am more than contrite and ready to be a very good girl. Well, until the next time I get into trouble. ☺

Victoria: Lol I know exactly what you mean. I recently went out and bought a new wooden hairbrush, oval in shape, and it does exactly as you just described stings, then burns. I might have to lose that one. Lol.

JACK&JILL: Lol OK I have better go before I get into trouble. Bye, Victoria.

Victoria: Bye Jill.

JACK&JILL Left the chat room.

CHAPTER TWENTY TWO

Lisa sat on the train on the way home from work, looking at her phone and smiling fondly. John had sent her two pictures. The first was all yellow, and the second was all red.

Total nerd, she thought, smiling.

World Cup fever had truly started in her house. John had been looking forward to this tournament for ages, and now it was here. With the girls away for the summer, he had decided it would be a good couple of weeks to do another boot camp, but rather than anything too formal and strict, they would have some fun mixed in with their discipline.

So he came up with a set of rules.

Lisa took a moment to make sure she had them in the right order before she listed them in her head, just so she could keep an eye on John.

First there were Yellow Cards. Each offense or rule breakage would earn her one of these.

Then there were Red Cards. Major offenses could see her award a Red Card but also, if she earned two Yellow Cards in a single day, she also got a Red Card.

Earlier that morning, she had received her first Yellow Card. He had sent a Yellow Card and then a 2nd picture depicting a note book page which contained her name, then number 1, and a notation which read:

'Breakfast dish and coffee mug left in the lounge.'

She had protested saying that was a house rule, not one of her DD rules, but he said there was no such distinction between the rules. Rules were rules, and she had broken one.

So she had texted back

'ok.'

Not "Fine" as that, along with "whatever" and the "fbomb" were amongst their list of banned words.

So she had gone through the rest of the day without getting another Yellow or Red Card, which is not surprising considering she was at work. Lisa laughed out loud when at lunchtime; she received a text, declaring it was;

'Half Time.'

Now, just minutes from home, she had got two picture texts, and she waited for the third to find out what she had done to earn further punishment.

Her phone "Beeped," and she quickly opened the message. She had to admit it was fun and quite exciting and the thought of a spanking or two was not unduly worrying her. She had been so good lately, both she and John following their rules and the relationship had benefited, being stronger than ever, but she had missed the sting of his hand on her bottom. That would be taken care of tonight.

The familiar shiver ran through the body and the tingle between her legs. She squeezed her thighs together tightly to increase the sensation as she read the latest entry. She saw her name, the number 2 and the notation that read:

'Cleaned and ironed clothes SUPPOSED to be put away, found in a cupboard.'

A further notation read;

'PENALTY!'

Lisa knew enough about football to understand his thinking. The 'foul' she had committed could have been a straight red, but having already had a yellow he awarded her a second, achieving the red and adding a 'Penalty' was his way of adding an extra punishment.

She text back:

'OK, ignoring a cupboard is kind of putting them away, albeit the food cupboard. I was going to put those away properly when I got home, but do accept I should have done that last night. What is my punishment?'

This got the immediate reply;

'Three spankings and oral sex.'

Lisa smiled. She felt excited. The game element diffused any actual anger or annoyance and the 'fouls' were not that bad to warrant anything too stern, so she was looking forward to getting home.

Upon opening the door, the usual smells greeted her, freshly brewed coffee and dinner cooking in the kitchen. She could hear the sounds of a soccer match playing in the lounge, so she called out 'Hello,' poured herself a cup of coffee from the pot and went through to join her husband.

John was on the edge of his seat, eyes glued to the game. They did not even flicker from the screen as he turned his head to accept her kiss on the cheeks, his own lips doing some contorted, twisty thing as he air kissed her in return.

Lisa did not mind at all. In fact, it was nice to see him enjoying himself so avidly. Soccer and that computer war game he enjoys so much. Such concentration is rarely seen.

Well, she thought with a smile, *perhaps one other time and place, she sees it regularly. Perhaps again, tonight, if she played her cards right.*

She sat back; just happy to relax, to be in his company and enjoy her coffee. The heat of the liquid eased into her tensions, soothing them away. Her own thoughts were interrupted by a loud whistle from the TV.

'Half time,' John announced as he sprung up.

'Get your clothes off and in the corner whilst I check on dinner.'

Lisa's pulse jumped, but she also felt a little aggrieved. Where was the romance, the tease? She had not expected this rather abrupt instruction.

John came back in and saw Lisa had not moved. He had only taken seconds to dash into the kitchen and back again. The look on Lisa's face dampened his ardour sufficiently for his bigger head, though partially devoid of blood at that moment, to think. He sat on the sofa next to her and took her hand.

'Sorry,' he said, 'that was far too brisk, see; we have twenty minutes before the match starts again, and I got a bit excited.'

Lisa smiled at his boyish face and flushed cheeks.

'Well, we had better get cracking then,' she said, cupping his face in her hands and kissing him on the lips. She sprung up and threw off her clothes. As it was summer she was not wearing that much, her skirt flew over the back of the sofa, the blouse followed suit, her bra ended up perched on John's head and her panties, they ended up down the back of the sofa, somehow, only to be found by their eldest daughter weeks later. But that is another story and another punishment; as John had not been so impressed with the thoroughness of her cleaning skills.

So, in a record breaking strip, Lisa now stood naked in front of John, hands on head, whilst John just sat and stared at her. After a few moments, Lisa blushed under his intense gaze and she gave an, 'uh um,' cough to get his attention.

John looked up and blushed slightly.

'God, you're sexy,' he said, his voice gruff with desire and emotion.

'Thanks,' Lisa said delightfully and gave a wiggle of her hips.

John growled and reached up for Lisa, who quickly went to him and over his lap without any guidance from him at all.

John paused for a moment to look at Lisa's lovely spankable bottom before he remembered the time and started to spank her. As his hand fell quickly, firmly, seeking to deliver a good sting to her cheeks. He told her of her offense, leaving the breakfast dishes in the lounge and not returning them to the kitchen as per her rules, as he smacked her cheeks, alternating between one and the other.

Lisa luxuriated under his stinging spanks; she felt all her muscles relax; all her work thoughts and troubles disappear as she lay over his lap. He had her; he was in charge and would see no harm came to her; he loved her and cared for her. The spanks stung, and she welcomed them. She did not feel punished really, though it was not quite a good girl spanking either, though she could feel herself getting wet, her lips tingling, demanding some attention. No, these smacks were somewhere in the middle, more a chastisement, a rebuke perhaps.

The spanking continued.

She smiled at her thoughts; a tinge of redness blushed her face as she pictured herself over his knee. No matter how many times she had been spanked since starting DD, those initial moments were always embarrassing.

The spanking continued.

Her bottom was stinging now. Each spank smarted immediately, adding its heat to the fire already burning her cheeks. Her legs kicked and soft, 'ows' and 'ouchs,' punctuated the air.

Ok, so quite a stern rebuke perhaps, she thought as the spanking continued. *Surely he didn't plan to spank her for the whole soccer interval.*

She became aware of his hardness beneath her stomach and deliberately moved her tummy around as he spanked her. She felt him try to move her, to relieve the pressure her body was placing on him, but she resisted and even the frantic flurry of hand spanks over her bottom failed to dampen her satisfaction as she felt his hot wetness against her skin. She felt his nails as his fingers dug into her bottom as he came, their pin point stabbing a counterpoint to the overall sting that suffused her cheeks and she loved it and it aroused her enormously.

She playfully wriggled her bottom, which caused him to leap from the sofa; he was always so sensitive after cumming. She would have laughed too if she had not been so unceremoniously dumped on the floor, right on her sore butt, too.

John helped her to her knees, as she ruefully rubbed her butt, laughing. John's face was full of concern before he too was laughing and pointing out she got exactly what she deserved for "that!"

Lisa tried to maintain an air of innocence, but the twinkle in her eye and wicked grin on her face gave lie to her words of protest. John hugged her tight, gave her another smack on her behind and told her to, 'Fetch a beer.'

Lisa gathered up her clothes, but John declared she would remain naked for the rest of the evening, so she just piled them up on a chair and padded barefoot into the kitchen to fetch her man a beer. She knew enough about the soccer match schedule to know there was a one hour gap between games, so she knew her next spanking would come after dinner. She couldn't wait.

*

The week was pretty quiet after that first night, which was great for Lisa. Every Half Time in the match, if there was not a spanking to be delivered, John was between her thighs either giving her oral or 'baby dancing' as she thought of it now.

But today Lisa felt a little antsy, unsettled and a little wired. She got through the day ok, but on the way home she could feel the tension in her shoulders and her irritation levels mounting, so she decided to take some pre-emptive action. She text him just one word:

'FUCK.'

Within minutes she got a reply – first a simple picture, all yellow. Then a note book entry.

'LISA, 3, Foul Language.'

Lisa smiled happily but then was overcome with a sense of mischief and texted back,

'FUCK FUCK FUCK.'

It took a little while longer this time for John to reply and Lisa worried she had pushed it too far. But then the phoned buzzed, and she eagerly opened the mail. This time, there were four messages. Intrigued, the first was the expected Yellow Card, followed by the second, the expected Red Card and the word

'PENALTY.' written on it in big, bold words. The third was the notebook entry. *John really loved his games,* she thought, as she read:

'LISA, 4, Repeated Foul Language, Penalty awarded.'

Lisa assumed it would be the three spankings plus oral again like the first night, and she was pretty close to being right. Pretty close...

When she opened the fourth mail, her tummy fluttered a little.

'On the way home, buy a bar of ivory soap.'

Oh, she thought, she had seen chat about soap punishments before and had often thought of suggesting they try it but always chicken out. She remembered it too well from her childhood. Now she would have no choice.

Her phone beeped, alerting her to another mail, which she opened.

'I've wanted to try soap as a punishment for a while, so exciting ☺.'

Lisa sent him back a cheeky text to say,

'Glad you wanted to try it. You will have to let me know how that goes. Lol.'

She didn't have to wait long for a reply.

'*Ha ha, when I say I wanted to try it, I meant that in a "you try" it sort of way* ☺ *lol.*'

Lisa laughed and replied,

'*You're not funny.*'

This prompted his usual retort:

'*I am funny. So funny. I could go on stage.* ☺.'

Lisa smiled fondly and texted him a smiley face back.

CHAPTER TWENTY THREE

Lynette Joined the chat.

andy Joined the chat.

LISA Joined the chat.

andy: Hey, so I been grounded for the rest of this month with spankings happening every few days.

Lynette: Hi.

Lynette: Ouch.

andy: I've got a really strict girl friend.

Lynette: What did you do to deserve such a harsh punishment?

David joined the chat.

Sally joined the chat.

David: Andy - are you new here?

Sally: Morning.

Sally: Hi Lynette, David.

andy: I lied to her. And I had a little problem with my attempts at cleaning the bathroom, so she grounded me and promised me a good bruised butt.

Sally: Ouch.

Lynette: Yep, lying will get your butt blistered.

Sally: Perhaps with this, the lesson will have sunk through. ☺Lying is always bad.

Sally: Do you feel better though? Did u get after care?

andy Yes, much better, I love the DD aspect of our relationship and yes there was some 'after care' lol I'd better go, I have to clean the bathroom every day until she is satisfied I can do it right every time.

andy left the chat.

Peter Joined the chat.

Peter: Greetings all.

Lynette: Hi Peter.

Sally: Hi Peter.

Peter: How is everyone?

Pat: Fine.

Lynette: Sore!!!

Sally: A little off, but OK.

Pat: Awww, what happened?

Sally: Uh oh.

Peter: Lol One day Lynette you will tell me 'two days since my last spanking!' one day. . . .

Sally: Lol.

Lynette: After that one Peter, I'm good for a month!!

Peter: Was your HoH playing with his new toys again, Lynette?

Lynette: No, his favourite - the oar.

Lynette: Pat - I let the kid get to me & kinda pouted all day which ruined his afternoon.

Lynette: So he ruined my ability to sit.

Lynette: Just for the rest of the night. That was long enough, believe me.

Pat: Do you know how many swats you got? I usually count to myself, keeps my mind busy. . .

Lynette: I don't but considering the beautiful array of colours remaining behind, I'd say he used more than enough swats.

Sally: You poor thing.

Lynette: I'm not joking about not being able to sit last night.

Tina: Did you sleep standing?

Lynette: Slept on tummy.

Sally: Do you get it on the bare?

Lynette: Always on bare.

Lynette: He sits back to headboard and me across his lap.

Lynette: I usually sleep on my side, but that wasn't even comfortable last night.

Tina: Oh Lynette, feeling better now?

Lynette: I can sit - though still really sore.

Pat: Is it that dull pain?

Lynette: No, still a stingy pain.

Lynette: Today is maintenance day. I'm hoping he will let it pass.

Lynette: Yes, but catch up is not fun either.

Tina: Maintenance on top of a spanking. . . ouch.

Tina: Let's not talk about catch up.

Tina: Lynette, is he more lenient for Maintenance, if you have already had a spanking?

Lynette: He has let it pass if he felt the previous spanking was enough.

David: Had a 'nice' anniversary celebration last night.

Sally: Tempted to tell my hubby I need him to be stern today but don't want a repeat of yesterday.

Peter: If the need is within Sally, perhaps you should tell him, might be better in the long run.

David: Sally - didn't you ask for a spanking yesterday?

Sally: Yeah, but it was a shock lol.

Sally: Think so? It's just my nerves. Afraid I might be short with him.

Sally: Feeling shy.

Peter: Leave him a note Sally.

Sally: Maybe it would save me the frustration.

David: Tummy time, you said (explains it all very clearly).

Sally: Back.

Tina: I can't sleep on tummy, feel like I can't breathe.

Pat: There's no every time with Graham.

David: We celebrated our 1 yr DD anniversary last night - she's arrived as far as I'm concerned.

Tina: lol David go well?

Sally: That's great. ☺

Lynette: David got a bruise for his anniversary - she got a card. LOL.

Tina: LOL LOL.

 Pat: Lol.

David: Yeah - she didn't hold back (like she said) - but this morning I've got that slight tingle.

Pat: A man butt.

LISA: I got a spanking yesterday too, three in fact, which were all ok. The change up this time was I also got mouth soaped. YUK.

Tina: Oh Lisa, I hate soap.

Pat: What had you done to deserve three spankings and a mouth soaping?

David: Oh dear

Lynette: I have not had soap before, and never want it.

LISA: John decided we should have a World Cup Boot Camp. Yellow and Red Cards included.

David: Lol. Your HoH does like the details ☺ lol.

LISA: Lol. He so does. Well, it has been really good, first day I got three spankings and then nothing for the next three days.

Lynette: It's easier to take them seriously and to let go when the HoH is invested.

Pat: Inconsistency Lisa?

Lynette: Urg I hate inconsistency. If I need spanking, I want spanking.

LISA: lol Lynette. No, I just had not done anything to warrant spankings.

Pat: Urrrg tell us already lol.

LISA: lol Pat. Well, after a day at work, I felt I could do with a spanking. Help me loosen up, unwind you know?

Lynette: Yep.

Pat: Oh yes.

Sally: Been there.

LISA: ☺ ok so I sent him a text. One word 'FU*K.'

Lynette: Eeek an FBomb, ok, that would get me spanked for sure.

Pat: Ok, I can see where the spanking and soap comes from.

Sally: That was brave or foolish. I am not sure which. I'll go with both lol.

LISA: Well, I got a yellow card for that, but I felt a little mischievous. I sent a second text.

'FU*K 'FU*K 'FU*K.'

Lynette: Noooooo seriously? You REALLY did want a spanking and then some lol.

Sally: Gulp, I would never have done that.

LISA: Well, John knew it was more in play than anger, so he was ok with it, but it gave him the excuse to use soap for the first time in our DD.

Lynette: I have never had soap. What was it like?

LISA: Yuk, he used it dry, though did promise a serious offense would constitute a wet bar beforehand. I also had to count the 12 whacks with the paddle, and they had to be audible.

David: Like I said, he loves the details.

LISA: ☺ It was hard. I had to bite the soap to hold it in place and every time I counted, my tongue would slide over the bottom of the bar, which tasted horrible.

Sally: Did it sting? Make you feel sick?

LISA: Not really sick, sick, but it didn't taste nice and not something you would choose to have in your mouth.

David: So effective against using the FBomb in the future Lisa?

LISA: Yes, no doubt, not even in jest. ☺

Lynette: Guess we're all going to be good tih's today

David: Do you ever feel like you love your spouse so much you're going to burst?

Tina: Every day.

Lynette: LOL Yes. About as often as I want to strangle him.

Tina: Strangle before burst.

Tina: In a loving sort of way, of course. ☺

Lynette: I can't imagine life without him.

LISA: Me too, more so since we started DD. I would say even more than when we first met.

Pat: I worked hard to get that man and suffered a lot to keep him.

Sally: Doesn't mean we have to like it.

Tina: Well, sometimes I kind of do.

Sally: True.

David: But deep down I do and afterwards I feel very cared for.

Tina: That's the nice part, David.

Lynette: Oddly, I feel taken care of during too.

LISA: Me too, Lynette.

Tina: Me three.

Sally: Me four. ☺

LISA: Ok, time to go, lunch time over.

Sally: Bye Lisa.

Tina: Bye Lisa.

Lynette: Bye Lisa.

LISA: Left the chat.

CHAPTER TWENTY FOUR

Funnygirl joined the chat.

Pjs: Funnygirl wb.

LISA: Hi Funnygirl.

Catherine: Hi Funnygirl.

LISA: We are done being silly and will answer your questions.

LISA: Pjs do you have bedtime tonight?

MR.K: She does.

LISA: When is hers?

MR.K: 2am but I'm going to make it earlier.

LISA: 2am?

MR.K: Yeah.

Pjs: Earlier?

Catherine: Why are you changing it Mr K?

Catherine: Uh oh.

Catherine: Pjs did you know about this?

Pjs: No.

MR.K: No, she did not.

Catherine: uh oh.

MR.K: Yes. ☺

Catherine: Soooo Mr K. . . . .what did you decide the new bedtime will be? Colin gave me a bedtime for a while too, but he just removed it; finally!!

MR.K: Well, I want to talk to her for a little after I get off work, so we will decide then. I'm worried she is pushing herself too hard and not getting enough sleep.

Catherine: Hmmm, that's a nice reason! It's good to take time for each other. Mine was 9 pm, and hopefully will never come about again. . . . . . as long as I can keep him away from the antics I pull on chat.

Funnygirl: Omg, my phone died. Ok here it is; I decided to get a tattoo with some girl friends last week and my hubby keeps questioning me about how I spent $200 and didn't come home with even one bag and I have been trying my hardest to

184

cover it up but he called a few minutes ago extremely upset saying he was coming home early because we needed to talk and I am freezing the f**ker out.

LISA: OH LOOK FIGHTING WITH MY 19-YEAR-OLD DAUGHTER AGAIN!

Catherine: uh oh Funnygirl.

LISA: Dammmmmmm.

Catherine: Have you been in a DD relationship long?

LISA: How long have you been doing DD?

Pjs: Ohh wow.

LISA: Hey my question lol.

Catherine: Lol LISA.

Funnygirl: Like 3 months.

LISA: Oh long enough that you're toast.

Catherine: Where's the tattoo, if you don't mind saying?

LISA: How did you hide it?

LISA: $200. It can't be tiny.

LISA: Yeah, where?

Catherine: Is it the money or the tattoo he will be upset about?

Funnygirl: Avoided bathing suits.

Catherine: Sorry for the 20 questions.

Catherine: The tattoo doesn't happen to be his name with a big heart around it does it?

Funnygirl: Along my upper back.

Catherine: Or maybe a bull's eye on your booty.

Pjs: Haha Cath.

LISA: Idk what to say, really. I know I'm not helping, but.

LISA: This is a big one, and you lied and hid it.

Catherine: Have you had a lot of punishment spankings in your 3 months of DD?

Funnygirl: Lol No. Not that many. The tattoo is Chinese for one love.

Catherine: Are you sure it says one love??

Catherine: You never know with the Chinese symbol stuff.

LISA: You hope it says one love.

Funnygirl: I have never even been in any real trouble before.

LISA: Oh well, if you were gonna do it, you did it big.

Catherine: LISA!!!

LISA: Am I wrong??

LISA: Hey I tell it like it is.

Catherine: Ohhhh no, so that's what the freak out is about.

LISA: Can I ask how long you have been married?

Catherine: No lol.

Funnygirl: Just a year.

LISA: Do you have other tattoos? Does he like tattoos?

Catherine: Who brought up DD?

Catherine: You or him?

Funnygirl: I did, but no, I'm hiding the tattoo, not the money.

LISA: Yeah, but hiding it for a week makes it a bigger deal.

Catherine: Ppl say the first time is not that bad because the HOH is usually worried he will be too rough. . . . .that wasn't my case with Colin, he spanked the shit out of me. . . but maybe it'll be diff for you.

LISA: Oh and you talk about me!!

Catherine: lol LISA, Sorry, it's the truth too.

LISA: This is why I say confess.

Catherine: But you know what Funnygirl, this too shall pass.

Funnygirl: There's got to be some secret to ease up the punishment, right? He's PISSED and I'm not sure if he even knows?

Catherine: It's intimidating the first time, yes, but there's got to be a point in time where you get past it so you might as well pull the band aid now.

LISA: Nope; but he shouldn't spank you when he's angry.

GermanGirl: Lol Never!!

LISA: Why didn't you just tell him?

Funnygirl: Omg like that would make it better. I asked him about tattoos before and he flipped.

LISA: Oh, she left chat?

Catherine: And she's gone. . . . . 😟

LISA: Damn, I hope she comes back. I want to know how this turns out.

Catherine: Do you know I freaked out and hopped on a chat the first night I was going to get spanked? The person I chatted with was like 'oh honey, the first time is no biggie, just one spank usually' and so I relaxed only to find out Colin didn't care. It was the first time. He went to freaking town.

Catherine: And all I kept thinking is; 'I need to find that chat lady who lied!!!'

Catherine: lol.

Pjs: Hahaha Cath.

Catherine: Was I thinking about what I did wrong to deserve the punishment? Noooooo, all I thought about was that chat person! Lol.

LISA: Now fighting with husband. Great!!

GermanGirl: LOL!

Catherine: Don't see red LISA.

Catherine: Breathe!!!

LISA: We just took a month's step back!!!!!!

Catherine: Uh oh LISA.

LISA: Nope; I'm pissed.

Catherine: Uh oh.

Catherine: 😟.

LISA: He tells me to let him handle things, and he takes his damn time and then waits for other things to happen and I'm yelling.

Catherine: A pissed LISA is not a good LISA.

LISA: No, and right now I don't give a flying f@$%.

Catherine: Awww no, you're cussing and using the f bomb.

LISA: Then he says he would rather deal with me. Sure, because I'm the easy one to deal with, the kid is more of a challenge.

Catherine: Maybe you guys need to take a break from each other for an hour and come back together to talk it out. Walk away for a moment.

LISA: Yeah, well, he threw out a 'whatever' which is the same as the fbomb in my book and I am sick of having to drive this whole train.

LISA: Oh, I'm not talking to him; he went out to deal with the animals.

Pjs: Sorry, LISA.

Catherine: I'm sorry too.

LISA: The deal was the 19-year-old had to finish the dishes before she went to bed since 2pm this afternoon.

LISA: She tries to go to bed, I make her do it; she does a crap job and is fighting with her sister and my husband tells her to go to bed.

GermanGirl: Yikes.

Catherine: Yikes, you both need to be on the same page with the kids. He needs to back you up.

LISA: Let's not get up off your ass and check to see if the dishes are done.

LISA: He says what do you want me to do?

LISA: REALLY?

LISA: Check the dishes and make her do it right.

LISA: So I have made him go get the child and make sure she is doing it right.

LISA: Because the child knows I'm about to go postal.

Catherine: I'm thinking he will probably see the reason in everything you just said, but right now it's all heated. Then, when it calms down, you need to explain "what is easiest isn't always what's best".

LISA: What is the point in giving up control if you have to constantly tell him how to do it?

LISA: UGH!!!! RANT OVER.

LISA: Sorry.

Pjs: Haha not a problem LISA.

GermanGirl: You're fine lol. . . . . . . We all have our moments.

Catherine: If you kill him, you can always hide him in GermanGirls trunk.

LISA: Right.

GermanGirl: Hey! Laundry is bad enough.

Catherine: Lol Well, the dead man will be well dressed in clean clothes at least.

GermanGirl: If he finds a dead body, he might wonder why there is a man in my trunk lol.

LISA: I have 2 acres I can bury the body here.

Catherine: Hahaha.

Catherine: I'll keep that in mind.

LISA: Oh round 2, he comes in and starts talking loudly to my daughter. She is saying please don't yell. So we have gone backwards. Now he screams at the top of his lungs. NOW I'M YELLLING. Yeah, that's mature.

Catherine: ☺ 😅LISA.

Catherine: It's hard to be mature in the heat of the moment. Lord knows I'm not!

LISA: I am so done!

GermanGirl: ☺ 😅LISA.

LISA: He says go to your room. I said no. I rescind permission right now for DD. He says go. I said fine and I'm taking my friends with me and left with the laptop.

Catherine: lol LISA.

GermanGirl: lol LISA.

LISA: Sometimes this thing is just too much work.

Catherine: It's a freaking LOT of work for sure, LISA.

GermanGirl: See, mine forgets I have a phone with 4G when he said he's taking the laptop and changing the password.

LISA: Lol But this chat room is a pain on the phone.

GermanGirl: Yes, it is.

LISA: Brb.

LISA: I won't be on much longer. I'm sure once he is done, he will come in to talk.

LISA: This is 2 days in a row she has tried to wait me out and lost.

Catherine: ☺LISA we love you! You will get through this, just like you told me the other day. It sucks, it hurts, but it passes. You both need to calm down from this fight and talk it out. You both have bad habits you are trying to overcome.

LISA: Tell me about it.

Pjs: It will be okay. ☺ ☺

LISA: Lol.

CHAPTER TWENTY FIVE

Lisa was fuming. What was the point of anything? How many times had she been spanked since their last stumble, their last long talk about DD and the improvements they had both seen and felt? She felt tears but refused to let them come. No, she was NOT going to cry.

She was ready to pack it all in, the DD, the relationship, the lot.

That thought shocked her enough to sit her back and to explore whether she really felt that way or was it the heat of the moment.

She thought back to before DD, when their relationship was getting to the point she could no longer take it. She knew the problem was mostly internal, her unhappiness and unpleasantness went hand in hand. She had felt her control, her grip on the family, her grip on her work, was slipping away, that she had had to do it all and that John had no responsibilities, no control, little input. She thought about that and realised that had been unfair. John had given up his work to look after the house and the kids. He had managed it all, seemingly without effort, and it was resentment that had fuelled her anger. It had been her choice to wrestle some of the control back from John with regards the kids. They had argued about that when she demanded greater input into the decision making. Then she had got a promotion at work and found herself drowning again and spiralling out of control.

Lisa pulled out her laptop and opened her DD file where she had kept some comments she had connected with in CHAT.

*

Jack&Jill: My youngest fell asleep at 4:30pm yesterday and so he was up at 5am this morning so no morning maintenance as planned and I miss it. . . lol.

Tina: We talk about it all the time and both read a lot. We want to make sure that we keep it going because it has worked better than any counselling or anything we have tried.

Jack&Jill: After the last 4 weeks my kids have started going to him for things and permissions more than me. It has been an interesting transition that I don't think they even realized what was happening.

Goldie: Yes, we have the standard rules: respect safety etc but we also are trying to stop my yelling and cussing.

Branda: Yelling is much better now if I could get sh** out of my vocabulary I would be very happy

Branda: Which is good and bad for my red bottom lol.

Eagle: Yup. And yup!

Peter: Lol.

Peter: I used to think it was just a male fantasy to find a woman who desired to be punished for breaking rules.

Jack&Jill: No, it is definitely not just a male fantasy.

Sweets: I wanted to try it and after we did, I realized I didn't just want it; I needed it. I needed the feeling of love and security it brings as well.

Eagle: Same here.

Jack&Jill: Yes, but now we are just sad we didn't do this way earlier, would've have made the last 16 years less competitive.

Peter: I think you women are amazing to think outside the box, seeking something that will help improve aspects about yourselves for your own benefit and that of your relationships.

Peter: I have also learnt being a HoH is no easy thing.

Nicola: Nigel says it is like trying to direct a tornado.

Jack&Jill: I am realizing that too, we have had a lot of conversations and he is feeling more confident.

Nicola: We just always both wanted to be right and I would argue until he gave up just for the sake of winning whether I was right or (rarely) wrong lol.

JACK&JILL: Especially for us, we had such a rocky start. Had we been in a different dynamic at the time, it would've been very different.

Victoria: Absolutely. I think people that don't understand think of it as abuse or as 'men controlling women' but it really is a partnership.

Catherine: I have a very loud and controlling personality, but part of that is because I have always been insecure. Not only am feeling more secure, but my trust and respect for my husband has grown.

Pjs: This may be TMI but I usually have very erratic and emotional pms. This past month, with the spanking and everything, my hormones were way more balanced, and it was so much easier.

Pjs: We had just started spanking, and I didn't want to stop what we had started so I said just do it. I had no idea it would actually be a blessing in disguise.

GermanGirl: My hormones get nuts too. It's like I can see myself being nuts but can't control it. It was so nice to have someone else leading the charge, so to speak.

Eagle: For me, part of it was desperation. I couldn't and still can't stand stagnation in our marriage.

Nicola: Stagnation is a silent killer, I swear.

*

Lisa closed her laptop as big fat tear drops landed on the keyboard.

Electrocuted by teardrops, she thought, and laughed a little into her tissue.

She thought of how her relationship had changed since starting DD. She was happier. There was no question, and they were closer too, unarguably. Their friends kept asking what they were on or who they had seen to get themselves such a relationship. John had resumed control over the household activities, including the kids, leaving her to focus on work. She had felt centred and calmed by DD. Yes the spankings hurt, but they needed to. She needed that pain to funnel all her insecurities, doubts, guilt and bad behaviour into, like a huge furnace. After a spanking, the heat in her bottom consumed all those negative emotions and thoughts, leaving only positives. She opened her laptop again and pulled out another file.

*

Pat: Do you find it weird to get your ass spanked by a guy who worships you?

Tina: Not really, because I can be frustrating to him. It gives us both a way to forgive and forget instead of dwelling on it forever.

Pat: It's a real expression of love.

Tina: It shows he cares enough to make us work.

Pat: I agree with forgive and forget . . . and the spanking helps feeling forgiven.

Sandra: I brought it to him. I just told Mark that I wanted to talk and then explained what I needed. It took a while to get into it, including a restart three weeks ago when we finally moved forward properly, but it just takes a lot of communication.

Sandra: It leaves me feeling very settled and calm.
Catherine: Yeah, we seem to be pretty happy and settled with what we've got going on now. But hell, a few months ago I would have said we were really happy and settled the way things were then too, but adding in DD has made us both even happier than I think either of us initially expected.
Tina: I suppose it's a sign that all is as it should be. I got a very long, hard spanking. He spread it over three instalments from after dinner until bedtime. Today my bottom is still quite sore. . . and definitely still coloured. But, I feel great! I feel renewed, happy, and very content to be the best partner I can be. The harshness of the punishment resulted in an exponential leap in my admiration and respect for my Husband. One thing more. . . . I definitely felt the need and desire for the long punishment. . . I deserved it, but I sort of wanted it as well. . . . .but today I feel like the last thing I want to do is somehow invite another spanking on top of the raw butt I'm sporting now. So, I am happy but very careful to be on my very best behaviour.

Sandra: I'm glad you feel better for it. I feel like that after a very long punishment too.

Despite the differences among DD-ers there does seem to be some areas where we are all similar. Post punishment joy being one of them.

*

Lisa closed the laptop again. She felt calmer for having reminded herself of the reasons why she connected with DD in the first place and the benefits she too had felt and shared with the others in the chat room. She also felt a little guilty. She had given up control over the household and the kids to John, so really she should not have been chasing her daughter to do her chores. John should have and would have, if he had been left to it.

Lisa took a deep breath, calmer now, a bit miffed still, a little injured that John had not backed her parenting instead of contradicting her instructions.

When John walking into the room, Lisa looked up at him then back down at her lap. She felt the tension creep back into her shoulders, her ire rising again. She knew what he was going to say. She knew it would result in her being punished as she was positive that DD was the right thing for their relationship and wanted it to continue.

"It too shall pass. URG," Stupid comment even though it was her own.

'I'm sorry,' John said.

Lisa looked up sharply. She assumed he meant he was sorry he was going to have to punish her and opened her mouth to retort.

But John continued before she had a chance too.

'I should have checked with you before issuing instructions. If I had, I could have backed you up and we would have presented a united front. I also shouldn't have yelled. We have rules about that and they are for me as much as they are for you.'

196

Lisa was taken aback; she had not expected this at all. John looked so miserable she found herself going to him, hugging him and telling him that it's all alright. John hugged her back.

'I have to make amends, though,' John said. 'I broke our rules so, instead of going to the game on Saturday, I am going to take you to see that show you mentioned the other day.'

Lisa felt a flush of excitement. She had wanted to see this musical for months and now she was going on Saturday.

'But you have paid for the match tickets already,' she protested. 'We could see the show the following week.'

John shook his head.

'I have thought about this. The cost of the tickets and missing the match is my punishment. For this to work, I have to. I let things get so out of control, I have to accept the responsibilities that come with being the Head of House and this is my way of showing you that I too have consequences when I mess up.'

She gave John another hug with apologies for her own part. Yelling at the kids and at him were also rule breakages. John was happy to let those pass, feeling his part was the source of the problem, without which Lisa would not have found herself breaking rules.

Lisa thought about it for a moment but knew she needed her own punishment. She felt guilty for the part she had played and knew a good spanking would banish those feelings and leave her free and clear to enjoy the show on Saturday. Otherwise, it would eat away at her all week and spoil her treat.

John looked thoughtful, then nodded. He understood the need to atone, to clear the slate, and Lisa was able to do this through being spanked. He knew firsthand how happier she was after a spanking. He told her to undress and stand in the corner whilst he went to check on the girls. He returned within minutes, announcing they were in bed and the chores were done.

Lisa was standing naked in the corner, hands on head, feeling settled. Moments later she found herself over his lap, her bottom getting the spanking she needed. At one point, John had stopped seeking to give her only a mild rebuke, but she shot him a look that left him with no uncertainty that that would not do. And he did not disappoint.

Whilst he only gave her a hand spanking, it was hard and fast and had her kicking and squirming before long. And John continued, he loved her and would give her what she needed to be free of this night's mess, so she could feel renewed and refreshed.

When John finally stopped, Lisa's bottom felt like a furnace, a hot enough blaze to have extinguished her guilt.

They slept together afterwards in each other's arms.

CHAPTER TWENTY SIX

The following week.

Lisa stormed upstairs and into their bedroom, slamming the door behind her. She stood, breathing deeply, for a few minutes, her temper to abating, giving her to think. Immediately, she felt a little guilty for yelling at John. In all the years he had been doing their laundry, there had never been any problems before, so wasn't he allowed to make one mistake? Then she remembered just how much she had paid for that nightie and her anger surged again, though she had been careful not to mention *that* fact to John when she was yelling at him.

She spied the laptop on the bed.

I'll give him "Reflection Time", she thought and opened the lid.

*

LISA Joined the chat.

JACK&JILL: Hi LISA.

LISA: Hi Jack&Jill.

Goldie: Hi LISA.

Catherine: Hi LISA!

LISA: Hi Goldie, hi all.

Victoria: Hi LISA.

LISA: Just popped in for a few.

Catherine: Welcome back LISA!

LISA: Thanks.

JACK&JILL: We are just chatting about nothing and everything. Jump in.

LISA: I am actually on borrowed time. ☺ I was sent upstairs to cool off and reflect. . .

Catherine: How's that going for ya LISA?

LISA: So I thought I would reflect on the computer.

JACK&JILL: Uh oh what did u do?

GermanGirl: Lol LISA.

Catherine: Yes, let's reflect together!

LISA: Things are going just fine. . . Got into a bit of an argument with John and I must admit, I got carried away. .

JACK&JILL: Hahahahah.

LISA: That is what we are reflecting on.

JACK&JILL: Happens to the best of us.

LISA: Ain't that the truth.

Catherine: That's for sure! It's difficult when you are seeing red.

LISA: Actually poor guy. He does all of our laundry. How lucky am I?

JACK&JILL: My reflection is it's all the men's fault.

Catherine: Preach!

LISA: I went to change for the night and saw a tiny bleach mark on a NEW very expensive nightie.

LISA: And flipped out.

LISA: He apologized. . . . swore he didn't use bleach and I actually know that is true.

JACK&JILL: Oops

LISA: But I couldn't back down. Maybe I feel guilty about spending so much on sleepwear to begin with, but the things I called him ☹

Catherine: Oh LISA.

LISA: And let's not even discuss double trouble. . . .let us reflect.

Catherine: Once you get started, it is extremely hard to back down even if you happen to notice you are in the wrong.

JACK&JILL: Wrong??? who???

JACK&JILL: Us??? never!!!!!

Catherine: Hahaha

JACK&JILL: Lol

LISA: You know my philosophy; 'even when I am wrong I am right.'

JACK&JILL: That's funny. ☺

Catherine: I LOVE your philosophy.

LISA: Lol.

Goldie: This is Gary. Hijacked Goldie's computer.

Brenda: It's not nice to steal.

Goldie: I like to say I borrowed.

Brenda: Ha, because that is a valid excuse.

Brenda: Ooooor, you could give Goldie back her computer like the nice husband you are.

Goldie: I am so nice that I will give her some spanks tonight.

Brenda: Sigh. I stayed on because it was HoH free lol.

JACK&JILL: Lol.

Goldie: But, I will be a nice HoH for now and let Goldie have her computer back.

GermanGirl: Lol.

JACK&JILL: Lol.

Catherine: Lol.

JACK&JILL: LISA what have you reflected?

LISA: I have reflected that John f &*&* my nightie and I am pissed.

Catherine: Lol.

GermanGirl: Ohhhhhh.

LISA: And I hear John headed up to "discuss" what I have reflected upon.

LISA: 'LISA Tell me why we are here'. . . . UGH.

LISA: So I need to run and reflect. . . perhaps run is the operative word.

LISA: Lol.

JACK&JILL: Ahhhhh run.

JACK&JILL: Run run run.

Funnygirl Joined the chat.

JACK&JILL: FunnyGirl, you came back.

LISA: Oh, I am staying for this. Hang on; I'll nip into the bathroom.

Brenda: lol LISA. Welcome back Funnygirl.

Goldie: Hi FunnyGirl, how did it go with your Husband?

FunnyGirl: ☺ Better than expected, but still bad news for my bottom.

LISA: Well, seems like a fair result, FunnyGirl, considering you did get a tattoo and spend all that money without telling him.

FunnyGirl: I know. Funny thing is, he was relieved it was for a tattoo, not that he is very happy about that. He thought we had bought drugs and got high. Lol. Hence, relieved.

Brenda: Lol. You see, let a man think for a minute and they imagine the worse. Always best to tell them the truth, saves all that worry and stress.

FunnyGirl: I know. I feel worse about that than anything, really. He was talking to helplines for the 'tell tale' signs of drug use and everything. I probably didn't make it much better laughing ☹ (but it was funny ☺).

Goldie: Lol. You will both probably look back on it and laugh at some point down the line, but you are right, not the time to laugh when he is telling you off. Stokes the fire on your butt, if you know what I mean.

FunnyGirl: My bottom knows exactly what you mean. Though I think I had good reason for all my behaviours but he was not in total agreement.

LISA: What was your punishment, if you don't mind me asking?

Jack&Jill: Gets popcorn ☺

FunnyGirl: lol Jack&Jill. Well, he explained there were a couple of issues to deal with. First, we have a rule about not spending more than $100 without checking with the other first. Just a way we manage our budgets. I had refused to agree to a season long TV sports package which would have cost over $100, so I knew he would not agree to the tattoo out of revenge and then he would feel bad later. So I was really thinking of him when I chose not to ask beforehand.

LISA: Sounds perfectly reasonable to me. Sports. . . . Urg.

Jack&Jill. Well points for imagination. Did he see it your way?

FunnyGirl: No ☹ but that led to the next point. I spent the $200 out of his account. He was not best pleased about that either.

Goldie: FunnyGirl! You didn't? You took the money from his account?

Funnygirl: Well, I had a good reason and technically, I did not break our agreement about having access to his account. Not really. But he did not see that my way either. ☹

Jack&Jill: This is so good ☺

Brenda: Hush Jack&Jill, How did you see it FunnyGirl?

FunnyGirl: Lol Jack&Jill. Well, I have access to his account in case of emergencies.

LISA: I cannot see the emergency in having a tattoo FG?

Jack&Jill: Wait for it ☺

FunnyGirl: It was on sale! AND it was his last tattoo of the day, so I got a further discount if I did it right there and then. I was saving money, really. All my girlfriends agreed.

Jack&Jill: Priceless. How could he not see reason? Literally 'laughing out loud.'

LISA: I think your girlfriends were having you on FG.

Brenda: You might want to find new friends FG.

FunnyGirl: Well, in fairness to them, we were all pretty tipsy, so none of us were thinking that clearly. And lastly I didn't tell him I spent $200 from his account and I did not tell him what on. He went overdrawn. ☹

LISA: Oh my, you must have really got it.

FunnyGirl: Oh I did. Hand spanking for like, ages. Then the paddle and last I got six with the cane. He never uses the cane, so I know he was really pissed. He told me the cane was for all the stress and worry I put in through. Which kind of made me feel better, like I was truly forgiven and absolved.

Jack&Jill: Yes I can understand that, I feel the same way after a punishment, especially when I have caused my Hubby stress or worry.

Brenda: Me too.

LISA: Yes, me too.

Goldie: So all is good now between you two?

FunnyGirl: Couldn't be better. I love DD. Before, we would have yelled and argued and yelled some more. I would have been in floods of tears. He would be frustrated and stressed and eventually over like, a week, we would slowly let it go and be back together, but a little weaker, like the join is not as strong. Now, I feel we are back together again immediately and the join is stronger than ever. My Love is stronger, my respect and admiration for him is stronger. And the sex. . . . . well. ☺

LISA: OK I had better go. John is knocking on the door and now I feel guilty. I have made him worry about me being in here so long. Urg

GermanGirl: Lol. Bye.

LISA: Lol night guys.

*

Lisa just closed the laptop as John walked in. She could see him frown.

'So you were reflecting with your friends in the chat room,' he said matter-of-factly.

'Yes,' Lisa replied, feeling a little guilty about that.

John held up a bathroom cleaner bottle.

'Remember this?'

Lisa felt her tummy drop.

'Why?'

'Well, I remember last week you insisting on getting this cleaner out just before we went to bed because you saw some black mould in the corner of the shower cubicle.'

Lisa did remember. She also remembered she had been wearing her new nightie and felt her face colour.

'I remember how great you were in bed that night,' she said, dropping her face a little so she looked at him through her eyelashes.

John laughed.

'None of that, young lady.'

Well, he's laughing. That's a good sign, Lisa thought, entertaining the idea she might get away with her earlier behaviour if she could seduce him with her feminine wiles.

'Do you remember it or not?' John demanded, added his stern voice, though she could tell he was more relieved he had not ruined her garment than being cross with her.

'Yes,' she said in a small voice.

'And what ingredient is in this cleaner, Lisa?'

Lisa thought and dismissed the first three smart answers and went with honesty. She knew she was now in a mitigation defence. She had sworn, yelled and slammed the bedroom door, though she was hoping he might have missed that one. A tri factor punishment was one to be avoided at all costs. The last time, she had supported black and blue bruises for several days. She kept the smile off her face when she remembered how nice John had been to her afterward once he saw those bruises. She never told him she had grown to like them. Not only had they represent their commitment to DD, she saw them as a sort of badge of honour, not that she wanted to repeat the punishment to earn them again anytime soon.

'Well?'

Lisa jumped as her thoughts returned to the present moment.

'Bleach,' she admitted. 'I'm sorry John, I thought you had done it, but I should not have lost my temper and swore. I know that. I've been so good lately, really improving. You said so yourself.' She added, seeking some good will.

'I did, which is why I am so disappointed with you.'

John looked quite sad when he said that, shaking his head, which cut Lisa to the quick.

'I am sorry, John, really sorry.'

Lisa went quickly over to John and held him close.

He hugged her back. Lisa could not see the small smile on his face. He could act a little too.

'Right,' he said matter-of-factly as he held her at arm's length.

'Clothes off, and then you can go back and tell your friends what really happened. Then we will see about your punishment.'

Lisa blushed at his pronouncement and peeled off her clothing.

It's funny. She could strip off in front of him, teasing him as she exposed more of herself for sex, but for punishment. She always felt embarrassed, especially once fully nude. She had to resist the urge to cover herself.

Naked, she went back to the laptop and signed into the chat room.

*

LISA Joined the chat.

JACK&JILL: Hi LISA.

LISA: Hi Jack&Jill.

Goldie: Hi LISA.

Catherine: Hi LISA!

LISA: Hi Goldie, hi all.

Victoria: Hi LISA.

Catherine: So what happened, Lisa? Did you talk it out ok?

LISA 😬 We did. Turns out it was my own fault.

Victoria: Oh No Lisa.

Goldie: Crikey wouldn't want to be in your shoes.

JACK&JILL: What did he say? How did you find out it was your fault?

LISA: He remembered I had used a bathroom cleaner when I wore the nightie for the first time the other week. It has bleach in it. I must have got some on me by accident. 😟

Victoria: 😊 🐾LISA.

LISA: Thanks Victoria. Well, I have to go. John told me to sign back in to tell you I was at fault, not him. Now I am going to be punished.

JACK&JILL: He is not angry is he, he should not punish you mad.

LISA: Lol no, he seldom gets that angry, and he is right to punish me. Later I will be pleased and proud he did, right now URG. Lol.

LISA: Wish me luck.

LISA: Left the chat.

CHAPTER TWENTY SEVEN

'So you told him?' encouraged Lisa. She had been dying to hear this conversation for the last few days. Ever since Debs had text to say she had decided to throw caution to the wind and suggest they give DD a go as an attempt to save their marriage.

'I did,' confirmed Debbie, 'and we are...'

'WAIT!' interrupted Lisa. 'I want details and don't miss anything out.'

Lisa made herself comfy on the sofa, big glass of wine in hand and waited excitedly. She loved couples' stories, and this should be a good one.

'Ok, well let me begin from last weekend when I saw John spanking you.'

Lisa went red and muttered;

'Well, maybe not those details.'

'Well, that is really where it starts, Lisa. I was jealous. Actually jealous you were getting spanked, and it shocked me.'

'Jealous?' queried Lisa, intrigued.

'Yes, at first it was just sexy, watching you getting spanked but as John worked through the issues and then his concerns and the two of you seemed so connected, it was really something and made me want that with Jake. It made me realise I love Jake, and we were being idiots thinking the single life would be better for us both.'

'Well, duh,' said Lisa, 'I've been telling you that for a while now.'

'I know, but until you realise it for yourself, it's just what well-meaning friends say, but don't really know.'

Lisa accepted the well meaning rebuke.

'I was right all the same,' she retorted with a smile.

Debs saluted her with her wineglass and continued.

'So, after your spanking I told Jake how I felt about him, our marriage, how I wanted him, us more than anything and how I felt DD would help us get there.'

Lisa nodded.

'How did you tell him?' she prompted when Debbie paused to take another sip of wine.

Debbie smiled at Lisa's excitement.

'I printed off some blogs and chat room conversations to back up my thoughts, sat down with him and just told him.'

'Oh, wow. I could not have done that,' admitted Lisa. 'How did he react? What did he say?'

'Well, it wasn't easy, but at the same time, I didn't want Jake to get the wrong idea or only pay a cursory glance at the stuff I had printed out. I started by telling him I wanted to give the marriage another try, give us another try, that I loved him. He told me he was so happy to hear that and that he loved me too and wanted the marriage to work. He admitted being single again scared him.'

John stuck his head around the door, but before he could get a word out.

'Ssssshhhhh not now, go away.'

Lisa waved him back out the door. A small voice in her head said that might not have been as "respectful" as she should have been towards him, so she added a loud,

'Love you,' for good measure.

Debbie took a sip.

'So where was I?'

'Jealous, chat, you both want marriage to work, Jake fraidy cat of being single, go,' filled in Lisa.

Debbie laughed and continued.

'So, having set the ground work and knowing he wants to make a go of things too, I hit him with Domestic Discipline.'

'Hang on, you just came out and said Domestic Discipline?'

'Yep, I wanted to see if he knew the term, had any reaction to it.'

'I bet he looked blank as a piece of paper,' guessed Lisa.

'Who's telling this, you or me?' playfully scolded Debbie.

Lisa held up her hand in supplication and then gestured for Debbie to get on with it.

'He looked as blank as a piece of paper,' she said, sticking her tongue out at Lisa. 'So I had to explain about the terms; Head of House and Taken In Hand, about the concept of one person being in charge, taking the lead and the other following that lead, supporting it and respecting it.'

'Let me guess, still blank?' quipped Lisa.

Debbie just laughed.

'Of course, he's a man. You have to talk slow and have pictures to get a man to understand.'

Lisa laughed with a glance at the door, part of her thoughts teasing her with the probability of a spanking later for shooing John out the way she did.

'So I let him read the blogs I had printed off, which detailed the why Taken In Hands' desire Domestic Discipline, what it means to us, why we need it. I saw it as a test sitting there being respectful and submissive, letting him read it without me saying anything.'

'How long did you last?' laughed Lisa.

'About a minute, jeeesh he reads so slow. I pointed out particular bits to him I wanted him to note in particular. Honestly, I think it probably took longer with my help, but we don't have to tell him that.'

Lisa nodded, not wanting to stop the flow now they were at the good bit as she saw it.

'So, he gets to the part about spanking,' continued Debbie, 'and stops. He reckons he cannot spank me, cannot bring himself to hurt me. Which is fine. I was prepared for that. I pointed out to him I understood what I was asking from him, that I understood it was an unusual request, but I wanted and needed him to try.'

'Umpf, John never said any of that. I was over his knee and getting my butt tanned before the day was done,' Lisa muttered.

Debbie caught the sound of complaint in her voice.

'But wasn't that a good thing?'

'It was great; perfect really,' Lisa confessed. 'Just saying he could have hesitated; just a little.'

Debbie laughed, knowing exactly where Lisa was coming from.

'Well, you might feel a little better once you have heard it all. See, once I have countered the "I cannot hurt you" concern, he switched to "How can it be a punishment if you want it" tack? Again, I was ready for that. I told him I wanted the punishment to ease the feelings of guilt, stress, and to rein in my moods but also to feel his authority, his leadership, to know he would call me on my shit, stop me and deal with it. I showed him all the comments TiHs' have made in the chat rooms and the blogs, saying all the same things.'

'So was he convinced?' asked Lisa, glad that she had not had all this when she brought it to John. She felt lucky that he had taken to it so quickly.

'Well, he has said he will think about it. Urggh, we both know that means he will do nothing about it and hope I forget about it.'

'You never know, he may surprise you.'

'Yeh, right, the last time he surprised me, he promised he'd "tell me when." Those kinds of surprises I can do without.'

Lisa took a second, then realised what Debs meant and burst out laughing.

A second or two later, Debs joined in.

'So, since you had that chat, nothing since?'

'Nope, though he told me to make sure the bathroom was clean this morning. Do you think that was him being Head of Housey?'

'Could be. Have you done it?'

'Well, I wasn't going to, to see what he would do, and then I thought if he was trying to be HoH, I should. To show him I was serious and would obey, so I did. Then I text him to ask *"what happens if I don't do the bathroom today"* and he said *"guess you will have to do it tomorrow."* Jeesh and I got a headache from thinking about it all morning, for that!'

'Well' cautioned Lisa, 'be careful what you wish for. It's your butt that will pay for it.'

'True, but now I am fully switched on to the idea, I really want it,' bemoaned Debbie.

'I can appreciate that, but you have been thinking about DD for months. You only mentioned it to Jake a week ago. Give him time to catch up.'

Debs could see the point, but was still a little miffed. She was impatient to get things moving.

'AND you can start being more submissive, you know, doing little things for him, if he asks for something, like a beer, fetch it without bitching about it, that sort of thing.'

'OK, teach, I hear you, though he can fetch his own damn beer, I'm TiH not a Slave.'

Lisa laughed, holding her hands up in mock surrender.

'I'm just saying, there are things you could be doing whilst you wait.'

'Without the accountability, though, it seems a little empty. I tried that before remember. But I will try,' she added hurriedly as she could see Lisa drawing breath for another lecture.

Debs could see she would also have a DD Monitor in Lisa once she and Jake got started.

She couldn't wait.

CHAPTER TWENTY EIGHT

LISA Joined the chat.

Peter Joined the chat.

Peter: Hello LISA.

LISA: Hi Peter.

LISA: I think we've passed each other in chat a time or two, but have never had the pleasure of chatting with each other. How are you?

Peter: I am great, thank you, and you.

Peter: Your exploits are the topic of conversation. ☺

LISA: Hmmmmm, are they now?

Peter: Flowers and a balloon. ☺

LISA: Oh lol.

Peter: I think we have both commented on posts in forums as well.

Peter: Though it's been awhile since I took a look at that site. Might try and make the weekly chat tonight.

LISA: Yes, that would be fun. The timing is usually off for me, but I try to get on when I can.

Peter: I recall from reading back DD is fairly new for you, though.

Peter: How are you finding DD, all that you hoped it would be?

LISA: Umm, well, he's never done DD before, but he's always been dominant.

LISA: . . . . .Well, I would say dominant in a way and extent that I would allow and that wasn't very much, but I could always tell he was waiting for me to let him take more control but was giving me my time to get there.

LISA: All that I hoped it would be? Well, I didn't really even think of it much before it came to mind and when it did, I discussed it pretty quickly with John. I was doing a lot of self-reflecting at the time and came to some big personal realizations.

Peter: Are you finding DD is help you reach the 'you', you desire to become?

LISA: Overall, yes I am.

LISA: It's been more of an emotional rollercoaster than I expected, but overall I am much happier with myself, my contribution to my marriage, as well as John's.

Peter: Emotions are something I see mentioned a lot, vulnerability and the quick reaction to perceived lapses by their HoH.

Peter: Perhaps that would make a good topic for chat night.

LISA: Yeah, I think everyone could speak on that at length.

Peter: Emotions, how to recognise DD affected vulnerabilities, how to deal with them, communicate them, spot them (HoHs).

Peter: One of the hardest things to figure out seems to be when a spanking would be beneficial to aid emotions and when they can make them worse.

Peter: I have had stories reflecting both and one where it made it worse, but the grievance was the HoH had not pushed through and spanked her through that as well.

LISA: Yes, you know most of the times I've been punished it was because of simple rules I was breaking about taking care of myself. I could sit back and get that I shouldn't have done what I did, and that John was trying to help me take all of it more seriously. Then for the first time the other day I was overwhelmed from work stress, hectic schedules, etc and I snapped at John over a ruined nightie.

LISA: I was extremely disrespectful and when he pointed out that it was my fault and that it was hardly ruined, it was the smallest of small bleach marks, I felt like a big disappointment and super, super guilty.

Peter: And this led to the punishment that resulted in having to tie you down.

LISA: Yeah.

Peter: 🙂 😅

Peter: So looking back, you feel it was deserved and you are glad he took you to task as and when he did.

LISA: Yes, no doubts in my mind about that whatsoever, but in the moment my emotions were high and as he started to tie me down, I freaked out that I would perhaps resent him for pushing me so far.

Peter: So the tie down was at the start of the punishment not mid way as you were unable to lie still?

LISA: The tie down was in the beginning because I kept trying to excuse it away and didn't want to lie down to begin with. I felt that something big was about to happen with me to be honest and was a bit scared.

Peter: No resentment, though, looking back.

LISA: He saw it, and was telling me to trust him to only take it as far as he needed to. Then he tied me down, but was explaining at the same time that he's on my team, he isn't the enemy and didn't deserve me lashing out at him with all the support he shows me and by seeing my punishment through he was trying to show me he takes our relationship seriously and doesn't want me to feel bad (which I would have) days later for saying things that were so uncalled for.

LISA: No resentment at all, it clicked in my head about half way through that this is what we agreed to, he was holding up his end of our "deal" so to speak and I needed to learn better about how to keep myself in check. Words hurt and can cut deep, and I'm not always very mindful of that.

Peter: Nods, it's good to read Lisa, not being in a relationship and very much on the outside, looking in on DD, I have thoughts and ideas of how I would handle situations, but mostly I look to see whether DD works. I am always impressed with you women to be honest, so strong and so resilient.

LISA: I'm super impressed with everyone I've met in chat as well. When my emotions were at their highest a month in, I found this chat and am so thankful for it. The women are all super strong so they have that alike, but at the same time they are all extremely different from one another and don't judge but embrace each other's differences. It's a super supportive group.

LISA: By the way, I think some assumed the flowers and balloons were an apology from John, but really I think it was a way to tease me a little bit and also show how proud he is of how far we both have come. He wasn't hiding anything that happened. That night prior was the toughest we had experienced for both of us and we both came out the closest we've ever been.

Peter: I agree with you, I saw them as a playfulness, a way to reconnect, all forgiven and he loves you sort of thing.

LISA: exactly Peter ☺

LISA: I need to jet so that I don't break one of my rules this morning. I don't need to add on to the rules I already broke last night. 😲

Peter: Have a great day.

LISA: Nice chatting with you, hope you have a good one and I can catch you on grp chat later

LISA: Yes, definitely, take care, sweetie.

Victoria Joined the chat.

LISA: Hi Victoria.

Victoria: Hi Lisa, how are you? Are you off?

LISA: Good thanks and you? Supposed to be, a couple more minutes won't hurt.

Victoria: Really good, thanks. Been chatting with Mike ALOT and we have had such a laugh together and our DD has gone from strength to strength.

LISA: That is great to hear Victoria; sounds like you too are growing pretty close.

Victoria: I think so too. I know I feel really close to him. He is something special in my life. I am always excited knowing we have a scheduled chat coming up, even though we text and mail all the time.

LISA: Sounds like romance in the air to me, Victoria. You mentioned your DD. How has that progressed?

Victoria: 😶 I'm starting to think of it as a romance to be honest but trying to keep my feet on the ground at the same time. DD, I've had to write in my journal 3 times in the last, like 4-5 days, because I keep snapping at Anne and on Saturday I dug my feet in over my chores. Ugh. . . I think I'm psyching myself out over summer break that officially starts on Friday.

LISA: Of course, if Anne is home for the school holidays, you won't be able to Skype with Mike as much, certainly not deal with your maintenance, punishment and stress relief needs.

Victoria: I know 🙁 it will be more corner time, lines and essays. Urg.

Tanya: Joined the chat.

Victoria: Hi Tanya.

LISA: Hello Tanya, welcome back.

Tanya: Hi guys.

LISA: Been a while Tanya, how are things?

Tanya: Really good, actually. Spent the weekend at my g/fs folks' place, which was an experience. 🙂

LISA: I sense a tale to tell Tanya, happy to share?

Tanya: Lol. Several actually LISA and sure, happy to share. The first part is that we travelled up on the Saturday and stopped in their local town for lunch before going on to her folks' place.

It was a nice little family restaurant. Now, I should add, I was really nervous about staying with her folks. It's not the first time we have met and I am not sure they really like me, worse my g/f chats about our DD lifestyle with her Mom openly, in front of her Dad and everything. So embarrassing.

Victoria: I would just die if that happened to me, Tanya.

Tanya: I know right. So there we are in the restaurant and I'm all fidgety and nervous and I say something stupid about her mom. I cannot even remember what it is, but Carol (my g/f) was not happy.

Victoria: Uh oh.

Tanya: 😟🤐 She said something to the waitress who came back a couple of minutes later and Carol took me by my hand and led me to the ladies' washrooms out back.

Tanya: The waitress said we had 5 minutes and as we went in, she sat down outside the door. Well, there was this bench running down the middle of the room, which was surprisingly large and spacious for the size of the restaurant. Anyhow, Carol informed me that she was going to spank me. That it was not only for my rudeness but also to settle me as I was clearly nervous.

Victoria: OMG.

Tanya: I know right, I said no way and stamped my foot and immediately felt like a kid, but she was firm and said we only had about four minutes left of privacy before the waitress let others use the restroom.

Tanya: Then she told me to trust her, that it was for my own good and I would feel better afterwards. She was so calm and self assured, before I really knew it, I was laying over her lap feeling my panties sliding down my legs.

Needless to say, I got my spanking. She had our spanking hairbrush in her purse!

LISA: Did you feel better afterwards?

Tanya: Yes, I did, I always do. Carol was right. I felt calm and centred. Carol insisted on holding my hand as we left, which I thought was sweet at the time. Of course, the waitress was grinning from ear to ear as we walked out. She had clearly heard everything. It was only when we passed another woman leading by the hand a younger girl who I assume was her daughter, not much younger than me, did I realise the significance of the hand holding. I felt myself go three shades of red and I felt a wave of heat wash through me. And I saw the waitress leave her seat, so the privacy we had been given was not the usual practice. Anyone can walk in and witness the spanking it seems, only Carol made sure that wouldn't happen to us. And to add insult to injury, Carol docked the $20 she had to tip the waitress to sit outside from my allowance.

Victoria: I am not sure I understand.

LISA: I think I do. I have chatted with other women who have tales of being spanked by their Moms or Aunts in restaurants or in Church. Usually in the bathrooms or a room set aside specifically for that purpose. When Carol insisted on leading Tanya by the hand, it was to show the other customers she was going to be spanked.

Tanya: 😊 😊 exactly.

Victoria: May I ask how old you are and your g/f?

Tanya: I am 23, Carol is 35. I know it sounds totally unacceptable, but where she was raised, it is totally normal. You would think I would end the relationship on the spot, right?

Victoria: Right, I would have.

Tanya: I know, but when Carol explained to me that she had last been spanked there. When she had told her Mom about our relationship, her mom spanked her 'one last time to remember her mom's lessons' and that she wanted to share that experience with me, at least in part (when she was spanked there were other women and girls who were in the bathroom or came in and all stayed to watch, totally normal, everyday occurrence, is how she tells it.) I felt a connection that had not been here before.

Victoria: ummm, I'm not sure that would have been enough for me.

Tanya: It's hard to explain, really. Maybe it's the age thing, but I was kind of jealous of Carol's life before she met me, a part of her that I would never be a part of. Well, getting spanked as she was spanked growing up bridged that gap for me. Crazy as it sounds, and it sounds just as crazy to me. Believe me, I think I fell a little deeper in love with her that day.

LISA: That is good to hear. Embarrassing as it clearly was. Carol was clearly looking out for you. She made sure you had privacy, and the spanking calmed you for meeting her parents and bridged the gap you just mentioned. Had you ever told her of your jealously.

Tanya: I had, only the week before when she was telling me tales of her growing up. Wow, I had not thought she might have done it for that purpose. Do you really think she might have done?

LISA: For sure. Otherwise, why stop in the town for lunch and not drive directly to her folks' place?

Tanya: 😊 😌 ohh thank you for pointing that out. I feel all warm inside. 😊

LISA: My pleasure.

Victoria: That does sound nice. NOT that I want Mike spanking me in restaurants but I can see how that would be sort of romantic, in a DD way lol.

LISA: lol Victoria.

Tanya: I feel a little guilty now. Just a little ☺

LISA: How so?

Tanya: Well, you remember I said Carol discusses our DD with her mom, well she told her all about our restaurant visit, of course, with me sitting there, face on fire. BUT it seemed to mellow her Mom towards me. After she heard that she was really nice to me and we got on really well.

LISA: And you feel guilty about that?

Tanya: lol No, not that. That night Carol and I were having sex, and it was 'wow' what can I say and I was a little vocal in my enjoyment 😳 So much so Carol had to come back up and put her hand over my mouth and finish the job with her other hand. (Sorry if that is too much information).

LISA: Not for me ☺ lol.

Victoria: bad LISA.

LISA: ☺

Tanya: lol well the following morning, her Mom was all, 'you two were clearly enjoying yourself last night.' And, 'one of you got a good seeing too,' which I found really funny and in no way embarrassing. Tanya, however. . . Beetroot. She has no problem discussing my punishments but sex, totally mortifying for her to discuss with her Mom. HaHa.

Her Mom and I had a great laugh together, Carol was not so happy.

Victoria: lol Sounds like you and her Mom really got on, in the end. Did Carol punish you for her embarrassment?

Tanya: We really did. It turned out to be a really good visit and I have no worries about going back there again now.

Punishment, not really. I have to give her oral on demand until I make her as noisy as I was that night. ☺

Victoria: lol, so a pleasurable punishment then. ☺

Tanya: Absolutely. It might last awhile too. Ssshhh don't tell, but I did sort of overdo it that night. Just a little bit. Whilst she was totally embarrassed with all the noise I made, she is also a little impressed with herself. The other night, when I didn't make nearly as much noise, she commented that maybe she needed to take me back to that restaurant.

I was very vocal the following morning ☺

Victoria: lol.

LISA: lol.

LISA: I had better get going. Thank you so much for sharing your adventures Tanya, great story ☺

Tanya: Anytime. Bye.

Victoria: Bye Lisa.

Lisa left the chat.

CHAPTER TWENTY NINE

Lisa lay over John's lap kicking her feet and promising to be good; to do things right away.

Her bottom blazed as the wooden hairbrush tanned her hide.

Why had she bought that thing? She asked herself for the 20th time that session as she, 'Owied', and 'Ouched' and begged him to stop.

Procrastination. So many of the TiHs had that as one of their rules. Lisa thought it would be a good idea to add it to hers. She knew it was a good rule, but right now, she was thinking it was not such a good idea. And she had bought the bloody brush, too.

I must be nuts, she thought.

*

She knew all the other TiHs had bought WADS before, "Weapons of Arse Destruction" so she was not unique in that regard, but once again she questioned her judgement. Out shopping, she sees a hairbrush. A nice innocent looking wooden, oval-shaped hairbrush, and her first thought her brains "go to" place was, *what would that would feel like on her butt!*

She should have checked herself into the crazy ward right then and there.

*

Now she knew; it felt painful. Not happy with its initial sting, the nasty hairbrush adds a deeper burn as a follow up. And she had told John not to spank her, as that evening they had their daughter's recital and they always used those hard wooden chairs which were uncomfortable at the best of times.

Had he listened, had in taken any of that into account? No, she had put off ironing her daughter's clothes until the last minute, sending the child into an apoplectic melt down. God, that child could throw a tantrum. No idea where she got that from, must be from John's side for sure.

And now she was paying the price. John had paid no heed to her pleas for leniency. It did not matter that it had taken less than five minutes to iron the blouse and skirt. She had left it to the last minute, had procrastinated. Oh, how she was coming to hate that word and, therefore, would be spanked. They didn't even have time for any hand spanking to warm up. No; it was straight over his knee, skirt up, panties down, and fire rained down on her butt.

She pushed herself off John's lap at his instruction and immediately rubbed her punished backside frantically.

One minute, that's all it had been, one minute of constant, very firm, hairbrush spanking,

Why had she bought that thing? It was evil, she thought for the 21st time.

The recital had been wonderful, and it would have been a perfect evening if her bottom had not protested throughout at the hardness of the chairs. No matter how she shifted and moved, there was no comfy position. She should have felt miserable, sorry for herself really, and there was a very small part of her that did, but mainly she felt happy. Happy her daughter was up on stage playing so wonderfully. Happy that her husband loved and cared for her so much that he did not hesitate to take her over his knee and apply the necessary punishment; happy that he had not been dissuaded from his intent; happy that she had such a wonderful family, such a wonderful life. She sat and basked in that for a second before she let out a soft, 'ow' as her left cheek stung. She shifted her weight to the right cheek, but that stung, so she just had to sit there evenly balanced and suffer her punishment. If anyone else knew, they would wonder why she was smiling.

As the recital drew to its close, Lisa was the first to her feet, clapping and cheering.

The other parents in front jumped out of the skins, such was her explosion of applause and cheer. The music came to its natural end a second or two later and the other parents rose and applauded.

Lisa was the last to sit down. There were many, many other students to play their piece that evening, and Lisa intended to give them all a standing ovation.

*

Lisa and John were soon in bed, kissing and cuddling. Both of them were feeling the warm glow of love for their girls, each other, the family life they had. Lisa slid over the top of John, straddling him; feeling his hardness against her lips. She ground her hips, rubbing her sex against his shaft, causing him to moan before lifting herself up slightly, reaching beneath and taking hold of his length, which caused another groan, quickly followed by a longer moan as she guided him inside her. Leaning down, she kissed John passionately as she slowly lowered herself down. Then she moved, slowly at first, getting used to his size within her, then faster. No games or teasing tonight. She needed him inside, needed to connect. She moved faster.

She slid her hand down between them and stroked her clitoris. Bringing her arousal up to the level John was already at. This was not going to take long for either of them. They both needed a "quickie" before going to sleep, neither having the energy for much more.

Lisa's arousal grew, climbing fast. John had his determined look on his face and she knew he was ready to fire but was holding on, just for her to catch up. He didn't have to wait long as she bucked and rode him hard as her climax took control and rocketed through her body, hard, fast and very, very, nice.

She felt him explode within her, warm, gooey, and lovely. She collapsed fully on top of him and lay cuddled up.

She felt emotional. So strong were her feelings at the moment. She felt the warmth of his love in her heart and within her core, and suddenly she knew she was pregnant. She would never be able to convince anyone but John that she knew right then at that moment, when her love for John had been all-encompassing she had felt a small tiny warmth, separate from hers but combined with hers, within her and she knew. That was her baby, alive and inside of her, sharing their love together for the same man.

She hugged John tight and looked up into his eyes, which were wet with unshed tears just like hers.

'How are you both?' he whispered.

'Fine,' she whispered back before the tears fell.

John held her tight, his cheek on hers, his tears mingled with hers as they both lay in pure bliss together.

Finally, after a while, Lisa had to know, had to ask,

'How did you know?'

John looked into her eyes, something he did so often now, so connected they were these days.

'Honestly, I couldn't say. But I just felt something, such a strong positive sense of love and completeness. I knew it had to be our daughter.'

'It could be a boy, you know,' Lisa said, a smile on her face.

'No,' he said positively, 'it's a girl, I can feel it.'

In the months to come, no one would believe they knew they were pregnant on the day of conception, nor the sex, as they proudly held their new baby daughter nine months later.

Lisa let out a giggle and cried out, 'Ride em cowboy, Yee ha!'

And they both laughed, hugged and kissed at the dual outraged cry of,

'Mooooom!'

THE END

AMAZON REVIEWS.

As a self-published author, your feedback is so important to me personally, and to opening up the world of Domestic Discipline to others.

If you could leave a review, I would really appreciate it.

L

© 2015 Lisa Simons

Contact
Lisasimons65@yahoo.com